The Chronicles of Kerrigan Sequel

Second Chance

Book 3
By
W.J. May

Copyright 2017 by W.J. May

This e-book is licensed for your personal enjoyment only. This e-book may not be re-sold or given away to other people. If you would like to share this book with another person, please purchase an additional copy for each recipient. If you're reading this book and did not purchase it, or it was not purchased for your use only, then please return to Smashwords.com and purchase your own copy. Thank you for respecting the hard work of the author.

All rights reserved. No part of this publication may be reproduced, stored in or introduced into a retrieval system, or transmitted, in any form, or by any means (electronic, mechanical, photocopying, recording, or otherwise) without the prior written permission of both the copyright owner and the above publisher of this book.

This is a work of fiction. Names, characters, places, brands, media, and incidents are either the product of the author's imagination or are used fictitiously. Any resemblance to actual person, living or dead, events, or locales is entirely coincidental. The author acknowledges the trademarked status and trademark owners of various products referenced in this work of fiction, which have been used without permission. The publication/use of these trademarks is not authorized, associated with, or sponsored by the trademark owners.

All rights reserved.
Copyright 2017 by W.J. May
Cover design by: Book Cover by Design

No part of this book may be used or reproduced in any manner whatsoever without written permission, except in the case of brief quotations embodied in articles and reviews.

Have You Read the C.o.K Prequel Series?

A Sub-Series of the Chronicles of Kerrigan.
A prequel on how Simon Kerrigan met Beth!!
Download for FREE:

PREQUEL –
- Christmas Before the Magic
- Question the Darkness
- Into the Darkness
- Fight the Darkness
- Alone the Darkness
- Lost the Darkness

The Chronicles of Kerrigan

Book I - *Rae of Hope* is FREE!
  Book Trailer:
  http://www.youtube.com/watch?v=gILAwXxx8MU
  Book II - *Dark Nebula*
  Book Trailer:
  http://www.youtube.com/watch?v=Ca24STi_bFM
  Book III - *House of Cards*
  Book IV - *Royal Tea*
  Book V - *Under Fire*
  Book VI - *End in Sight*
  Book VII – *Hidden Darkness*
  Book VIII – *Twisted Together*
  Book IX – *Mark of Fate*
  Book X – *Strength & Power*
  Book XI – *Last One Standing*
  Book XII – *Rae of Light*

The Chronicles of Kerrigan SEQUEL

Matter of Time
   Time Piece
   Second Chance
   Glitch in Time
   Our Time
   Precious Time

Find W.J. May

Website:
http://www.wanitamay.yolasite.com
Facebook:
https://www.facebook.com/pages/Author-WJ-May-FAN-PAGE/141170442608149
Newsletter:
SIGN UP FOR W.J. May's Newsletter to find out about new releases, updates, cover reveals and even freebies!
http://eepurl.com/97aYf

SECOND CHANCE

Description

Second Chance
The Chronicles of Kerrigan Sequel #3

The highly anticipated Sequel to the Chronicles of Kerrigan series, by international bestselling author, W.J. May.

'Take me to the time when things were fine, it's all broken now.' The Maine

A little persuasion goes a long way...

Rae Kerrigan thought that her father's trial was going to be the single most defining moment of her life. Little did she know, the trial was only the beginning.

The tatu world erupts in chaos as a surprising new villain begins to emerge. One with the power to take down even the great Rae Kerrigan with nothing more than a few simple words.

Still reeling from the attack and the heroic part Simon had to play, Rae finds herself facing a kind of enemy she's never encountered before. One that destroys from the inside-out.

Can Rae and her friends find a solution in time? What part will Simon have to play?

Is there any bond strong enough that it can't be broken?

Chapter 1

"Time heals all wounds."
Well, not all of them...

The knife hit bone. It slid alongside it a ways. Then pulled back out— dark red.

With a broken gasp, Rae sank to her knees. Still staring up at the love of her life. Still completely unable to comprehend what had happened. Even with the blade still clutched in his hand, she couldn't bring herself to believe it was true. He hadn't just thrust a knife into her chest.

"D-Devon," she whimpered, crumpling onto the grass. "Dev..."

If this had happened a few weeks ago when she still had her immortality, she'd be okay. She still had the ability to heal most any wound in a mere matter of seconds. A stab to the chest would have been painful—excruciating actually. But it wouldn't have been fatal. It wouldn't have been something that she was unable to overcome.

But she didn't have that power anymore. She had given up immortality in exchange for a future with the man she loved. Given up the promise of eternity for a mortal life with a mortal man. The same man who had just threatened to end that life forever.

"Devon, what did you..."

The world around her blinked in and out of focus. As she lowered her forehead to the ground, she heard several screams— all of them offset with the steady *drip* of her blood pooling beneath the blade and the thumping of her heart echoing in her ears. In her blurry periphery, she saw a flash of crimson. She tried to lift her head.

Molly!

She cried out telepathically. If she could no longer trust the man she loved, at least she could count on the girl she thought of as a sister. Across the grass, the two of them locked eyes. Both terrified. Both completely unable to comprehend what had just happened. A high voice screamed something unintelligible, and in what felt like slow motion Molly began sprinting towards her...

...and then stopped.

Rae's brow creased in horror as the redhead suddenly skidded with her feet. Her bright blue eyes glassed over for a second. As distant as Devon's had been as he walked towards her. Then, without so much as a second glance, she took off running in the opposite direction.

"No," Rae gasped, staring after her as she tried to stem the bleeding.

As frantic as her efforts were, they weren't making much progress. The knife had hit either an artery or a major vein, because she was losing blood faster than she could stop it. Already, the edges of her vision began to blur as Molly got smaller and smaller, racing towards the horizon. Rae watched until she was just a tiny spot, soon swallowed by the trees.

Then a sudden shadow fell over her, and she gazed up in horror.

"Devon," she pleaded as he slowly walked forward.

Never in her life, not a single moment, had she been afraid of him until now. It was as if the curtain had fallen away. Suddenly, she could see what everyone else saw when they saw him.

Not the man who shared her bed. The same man who secretly despised pancakes, and even more secretly adored taking bubble baths with his fiancée when he thought no one was around.

He was a legend. The Privy Council's prized weapon. The man who would stop at nothing to get the job done, and had the talent to back it up.

The man who was about to kill her.

"Devon—please!" she whispered, trying to catch her breath. The crowd around her had begun to go wild, but strangely enough none of it had anything to do with her. They were all having their own problems. She just couldn't tell what those were. "It's me, Rae. Please..." she eyed the bloody knife still in his hand, and weakly scrambled back on the grass, "*don't!*"

"DEVON!"

Rae closed her eyes in momentary relief. Thank bloody goodness! She wasn't the only one who saw what was happening! This nightmare wasn't just hers alone!

Julian was racing forward, looking like he couldn't believe what he'd just seen.

His dark hair whipped against his pale face as he barreled towards them, angling his entire body between his two best friends as a shield. But before he could get within twenty yards, a giant swinging fist caught him right in the face and sent him flying backwards once again.

"...Mitch?"

Rae couldn't believe it. Guilder's own head of security. A man who virtually worshipped her and the rest of the group. Venerated them as 'war heroes' and vowed to protect them with his very life. The same man who'd carried Julian out of the factory the day of the battle, moving heaven and earth to keep him safe. *He* was the one who'd just knocked Julian unconscious.

For a split second, he turned towards her. Every muscle in his colossal body was tensed at the ready, but the look in his eyes was just like Devon's.

Vacant. Removed. Like someone had erased the man entirely and left a hollow vacuum in his place. It was the eyes...she could see it in the eyes.

Julian stirred on the ground, but didn't wake. Mitch was over two hundred pounds of pure muscle, and he'd struck him right in the temple.

But Julian wasn't the only one who saw what was really going on.

"RAE!"

Gabriel didn't scream for Devon's attention, but for hers. Despite the increasing madness around him—from the looks of things, the crowd had begun to turn on each other—he forced his way through, sprinting towards her as fast as he could.

She lifted a shaking hand. Looking out past Devon and the knife. Reaching towards him with every bit of strength she had left, willing him to get there in time.

But Gabriel, too, found himself waylaid by forces he could not have possibly predicted.

A slender hand shot out. Followed by a gust of white hair.

And just like that, Gabriel Alden—the warrior who could never be tamed—found himself frozen in place. At the mercy of his little sister, whose sapphire eyes were just as blank as Devon's.

"Angel..." His jaw clenched shut, but he forced a few final words, fighting off her tatù's numbing power as best he could. "W-What are y-you doing?!"

She contemplatively tilted her head to the side, but it was like she couldn't hear him. Like she was just going through the motions, acting on orders above and beyond herself.

"Angie, please," he tried again, locking into place all the while. "Please, don't—"

But then he could speak no more. He was deep in her clutches. A place that only Rae had ever been able to escape.

Angel stroked his hair with that same look of thoughtless unconcern and stood beside him. Guarding him, despite the fact that she was the one who put him there.

What the hell is going on?!

The ground shook and, despite her mounting blood loss, Rae was suddenly hyper-aware of the madness going on around her.

Jonah, the Privy Council agent who'd put up the force field, was still tenuously holding the crowd at bay, but the hordes of people were proving to be too much. Whatever temporary madness had come over Devon and Angel, it was clearly affecting the others as well. The stately grounds of Guilder Boarding School had become a battle ground as people of every age and level began openly using their powers against one another.

Water put out fire. Fire defeated wind. An isolated storm cloud was firing out bolts of lightning at everyone who was standing too close, and at least a quarter of the people who had come to hear Simon Kerrigan's sentencing suddenly shifted into wild creatures.

The noise was deafening. The chaos unrivaled by anything Rae had ever seen.

Except, her problems were more immediate than that. Her fiancé was still approaching. And he was still holding that deadly knife. Moving as if stuck in molasses, but coming closer nonetheless.

"Devon!" she screamed, with what little strength she had left. "Can you even hear me?!"

From the corner of her eye, she could see Luke racing towards her. But before he could get more than a few steps, he was struck in the side of the head by his own father. A second later Luke straightened up, drained of emotion as the two of them faced off against each other.

Father and son. Battling to the death.

"Devon—please! It's ME!"

She trusted him with her life and her heart. How could this be happening? Had he been pretending all along? Did he not love her? Was this all a plan, like Lanford? A new pain ripped through her heart. She shook her head, refusing to believe that this was happening.

"Devon—please stop!" A sob tore through her throat as she begged him.

There was a sudden explosion. It halted Devon's advancement toward her. Desperate, Rae looked around. Her parents, along with the Privy Council's second in command—Louis Keene—were instantly overrun by civilians as Jonah collapsed and the force field failed. With a mighty cry, both Beth and Simon were momentarily blocked from view. Their screams reached Rae's ears as they tried to get to her. A space broke through the crowd and Rae could see them standing back to back for protection, fighting side by side.

She dragged her gaze away to her fiancé.

In Devon's face there was not an ounce of mercy. Or compassion. Or recognition. Or any of several countless things that had come to define him.

He was like a hollow shell. Moving without feeling it. Looking down at her without feeling it. Lifting the knife without a single shred of emotion in his eyes.

"Devon!" Rae screamed as the blade glistened above her, hovering in the air. She stared, too weak to stop him, too lost to move. This was how it was going to end. After everything, Devon's hand would be the one to stop the Kerrigan line.

But the knife never came down.

Julian flew out of nowhere, tackling his best friend to the ground and sending the blade clattering out of his hands. Rae gasped and backed away farther, still trying her best to stem both the blood and the pain as the world around her began to flicker. She tried switching through a hundred different tatùs, anything that could possibly help her, but each of them failed. Whatever evil had descended upon the school, it had done well to take her out first. The blade had simply cut her too deep. A river of blood was pouring from her chest and it was all she could do to keep her eyes open.

Fortunately, there were others still standing ready to fight for her.

On the grass behind them, Rae saw Mitch Ford's body. His eyes were closed in peaceful slumber and both wrists were bound behind his back. Julian had recovered with a vengeance and taken out Ford himself, arriving just in time to stop Devon from doing the unthinkable.

"Dev—what the hell are you doing?!" he cried as the two of them scrambled back to their feet.

Whatever was happening to the people around them, Julian and Rae seemed completely unaffected. He was racing towards her now, pale with horror, numb with shock. His dark eyes as bright and clear as ever.

But he never should have turned his back on his friend.

Just a second before he could reach her Devon grabbed him by his trademark ponytail, yanking him backwards before hurling him into the ground.

Rae stifled another scream.

Julian cried out sharply as he hit the dirt, but rolled over automatically to get back onto his feet. Devon was standing in front of him, the knife clutched in his hand again.

"*Don't.*"

It was the only word he said. In a voice that sounded nothing like his own.

Julian's eyes widened in shock as he stared back at him. The man who had always been like a brother. Closer than a brother. The man he trusted above anyone else. "Devon...what are you doing?"

Rae clutched her chest and watched as Devon took a step forward, raising the blade threateningly.

"Get back, Julian. I don't want to hurt you," Devon whispered.

"...Don't want to *hurt* me?" Julian echoed, at a loss. His eyes flickered to Rae, making sure that she was still breathing, before returning to his friend. "Dev, you need to listen to me, okay? I need you to put the knife down. Give it to me." He took a tentative step forward. "It'll be okay, I promise. Just give me the—"

There was a blur of speed, followed by a sickening crunch. Then Julian was on his back. Another cry of pain echoed in the air.

Devon stared back impassively. "I said *don't*."

A stream of silent tears slipped down Rae's face. Her fingers and toes were beginning to feel cold. It felt like there was a steady weight being pressed against her.

"This isn't you," Julian panted, getting to his feet. "Dev, something's happened to you." He clutched at his shoulder as he pulled himself up. "Look around. Does any of this look right?"

Another blow, and he was back on the ground. The earth shook with the force of the impact. His best friend expertly preyed on the holes in his visions, giving him no time to slip into the future lest something happen to Rae.

"Jules...just get out of here," Rae murmured, still inching backward on the grass. While the pain may have been overriding her other senses, she was still hyper-aware of the fact that Devon still had a weapon in his hand. "He can't hear you. It's like he's not even here."

But Julian wasn't about to leave her. And he wasn't about to leave Devon.

"This isn't you," he panted, pulling himself up once more. A steady stream of blood was dripping down his arm, but he lifted it to point to Rae. "You love that girl. Love her more than anything in the whole world. You don't want to hurt her."

A boot came flying out of nowhere, and kicked him right in the jaw. Devon straightened and stared passively as he set his foot back down.

"Jules!" Rae screamed.

But he simply spat out a mouthful of blood and pulled himself up once more. Whether he was unwilling or unable to fight Devon—Rae would never know. All she knew was that, with every breath, Julian kept trying to stop him.

"Remember what you told me the first time you saw her? Back at Guilder?" Julian staggered to his feet and kept moving forward. "You said that you'd just met the most beautiful girl in the world. That you couldn't get her out of your head. That you didn't want to."

This time his eyes flashed white, and he dodged Devon's attack before it could land. There was a violent collision, so fast that Rae couldn't quite understand, then the two of them went flying in opposite directions, landing hard upon the grass. The knife dropped out of Devon's hand and he scrambled to grab it again.

"You don't want to hurt her. You don't want to hurt me." Julian wiped a smudge of blood from his face, angling himself between them. "You have to fight this—"

"I can't..." Devon faltered, then grew suddenly steady as he strode forward and picked up the knife from the ground. "I told you... don't. This isn't about you."

Rae's blood ran cold but Julian stayed steady, moving to stand right in front of her.

"Rae, are you okay?" he murmured, keeping a careful eye on Devon's approach all the while. "Say something, talk to me."

She nodded weakly and embraced the lie, knowing that her time was running out. "Yeah... I'm okay."

He hazarded a glanced behind him before turning his attention back to his partner, who was advancing with a cold look of determination in his eyes.

It was like they were sixteen years old again. Back in the Oratory, sparring with together just like they did every morning. Only this time the stakes were much, much higher.

"Dev, please." Julian raised his hands entreatingly. "You don't want to do this. It's *me*—"

A hard smack hit him right in the jaw. Followed by another.

Still, Julian stood firm.

"Please." His hair fell into his face, and he pushed it back with trembling hands. "You don't want to hurt her. I don't want to hurt you—"

There was another sudden impact, but this time it was Devon who went flying. Rae stifled a scream, and grabbed weakly at her ravaged skin as her fiancé came down hard upon the ground.

It was a foolish man who would pick a fight with a psychic. No matter how talented they might be. Even as the prophetic glow faded from Julian's eyes, a soft *snap* echoed across the noisy field.

Devon's arm had broken.

If only that would stop him...

"Come on, man! *Please*!" Julian cried as Devon surged forward again, as oblivious to the pain as he was to everything else. "Just listen—"

"It's you who isn't listening to me," Devon replied, dodging his friend's attack and ducking cleverly behind to catch him in a chokehold. "This isn't about you. It's only about *her*." His arm tightened as his eyes glassed over unfeelingly. "I told you not to get in my way."

"Devon, stop it!" Rae screamed as he squeezed even tighter. Julian's hands came up to free himself, but Devon was standing at such an angle that Julian couldn't break free.

The whole world was blacking out entirely for her, lost in a din of screams and sound, but out of the corner of her eye she saw a sudden stillness in the crowd. Like a black hole. A place that none of the madness or chaos had yet to trouble.

With tremendous effort, she raised her head to see a tiny brunette staring back at her. It took another second still to realize that it was Samantha standing motionless in the crowd.

For a split second, the two of them locked eyes.

It was utterly surreal. To be so motionless, in a field of pandemonium.

It was like time itself had stopped, and for a moment both girls just stood there. Frozen as they stared. One bleeding. One standing completely unmolested amidst the carnage.

Then a broken gasp brought Rae back to the present.

"Dev—" Julian choked, grasping desperately at his arm. The ashen edges of his face were already beginning to turn blue as his eyes drifted out of focus. "Dev, don't—"

"DEVON—*NO!*" Rae screamed.

It took every bit of effort she had, and the second she did she almost regretted it.

Devon did, in fact, stop. He released Julian, dropping him to the ground. But, in doing so, he turned his attention once again to her.

She started shaking with outright fear as he moved deliberately towards her.

"Honey," she began, her voice dropping to no more than a whisper, "what are you doing?"

He didn't even slow down.

"Devon, you need to fight this. Whatever it is, just..." She trailed off as her eyes flickered desperately around. Searching for anyone who could possibly help her. There weren't many options.

Luke and his father were still locked in a deadly game of cat and mouse. While Luke might not have been the one gifted with super speed, he had overcompensated by training to perfection with every weapon and method under the sun. Although the Commander had clearly gotten in a few devastating blows, Luke was already beginning to turn the tables.

Molly was long gone, and Gabriel still frozen—staring with wide eyes while Angel stood calmly beside him. Watching, but not seeing. Not registering anything except her specific task.

Kraigan was nowhere in sight. He had taken off right after the hearing.

"Mom!" Rae cried in desperation, backing away as best she could as her fiancé moved towards her with the blade. "Mom, where are you?!" She swiveled around desperately, but Beth was locked in her own battle and couldn't hear her daughter's cries. No fewer than thirty members of the crowd had descended upon her, and it was all she could do to hold her own. "...Dad?"

The word slipped out before Rae could stop it. But, as strange as it felt, every fiber in her body was praying for a response. She had stared into Devon's eyes, and found nothing familiar there. She knew in her heart of hearts that she was out of time, and out of options. Even if it meant calling upon her murderous father, she would take whatever help she could get.

And right at that moment... all her prayers were answered.

"Rae?"

She forced her chin up and saw Simon Kerrigan standing still amidst the crowd. Despite the band strapped around his anklet, the one stifling all his powers, he'd still remembered enough hand-to-hand training to make short work of those people swarming up around him. The Oratory had a way of seeping lessons into your skin. Imparting skills that time itself could never dull.

He lashed out with a vicious kick, and sent the last person lunging at him flying back towards the hills. Then, without a second's thought, he began sprinting towards his daughter.

Devon didn't notice. He was in a world all to himself. When he reached Rae, he sank slowly onto one knee—the same way he'd done when he proposed. He stared her up and down with those unfeeling, unblinking eyes. "I have to kill you now."

A single tear streaked down Rae's cheek as she shook her head, reaching for his hand in spite of herself. "No... you don't. Devon, please—this is me. Rae. The girl you're going to marry." An image of the two of them standing beneath the treehouse flashed behind her eyes, and she squeezed his cold, unyielding fingers. "I love you, Devon."

A glint of silver flashed through the air as he raised the blade behind his head.

Her breath caught suddenly in her chest as she stared at him, stunned into silence. *I can't believe it. After everything that's happened. This is how it ends? With Devon?* A hundred different emotions crashed through her all at once, but in the end she was left with just one overriding conclusion. *He's going to hate himself. This is going to kill him.* But even as she thought it, a flicker of light sparked suddenly in his eyes. His hand stopped its forward trajectory, like it had gotten stuck in thick mud. And for a split second, the curtain pulled back and Rae was able to see the devastation raging beneath.

"Rae," he whispered, fighting with every inch of himself, "*run!*"

But she couldn't.

And he couldn't stop himself either.

With a heartbreaking look of anguish, he lifted the knife once more and lurched to bring it down with all his strength upon her heart.

Except...

It never got there.

"Sorry, Wardell." Simon caught his wrist with a breathless gasp. "But that's my daughter."

Chapter 2

Rae watched in terrified awe as her father and her fiancé spun around to face one another.

Each frozen with rage. The knife glistening on the ground just behind Devon.

"Rae, honey? You okay?" Simon called, never taking his eyes off Devon.

Every instinct told her to just say 'yes,' but this time her body wouldn't have it. Even as she opened her mouth to try, a river of blood came to the surface and she coughed it to the ground.

"... Not so great." A sudden wave of pain and nausea crashed over her and she bent at the waist, cringing into the crimson grass. "Dad... please... hurry." She stared at her father and fiancé facing off in front of her. How much time did she have? Why wouldn't her tatù slow the flow of blood? What if she tried Angel's tatù and froze the flow? Would it work?

Simon cast her one stricken look of panic before turning back to Devon.

"Son, are you anywhere in there?" He read Devon's blank stare with an expert gaze, and then nodded grimly. "In that case, trust me. You'll thank me for this later."

Rae didn't know if it was the blood loss, or if her father had really moved that fast. But the next thing she knew he was flying in the air—streaking towards her fiancé with a skill that she had only ever seen in Devon himself. A second later his boot landed squarely on Devon's chest, and the younger man somersaulted backwards across the ground, rolling to a painful stop upon the grass.

For most anyone else, that would have been the ballgame. It was a fight-ending blow delivered with unspeakable force. But Devon had never been one to give up easily. Already, he had recovered the blade and was angrily surging forward. "Simon," he spat. He seemed to recognize Simon, even amidst his stupor. "This is a long time coming."

Simon's lips twitched up in a humorless smile, while he angled defensively against the grass. "Like father, like son."

With a vicious cry Devon launched himself in the air and flipped twice, blurring into a streak of light and color as he came down on Simon. It was an extraordinary attack. The kind that, no matter how prepared you were, there was no way to fight against. Even in her trance-like state, Rae could hear bones snapping as her father hit the ground. He lay there for a minute, recovering his senses, before spitting out a mouthful of blood and pushing to his feet.

"Like I said. You're just like your father."

There was no response. Devon was past that now. His hollow eyes focused only on the task that lay ahead. Rae choked on a frightened scream as he made his way towards her once again.

Except he never got to her.

There are few things more powerful than a father's love, than a man's desire to protect his children at all costs. Simon may have been away for the better part of twenty years, but one way or another he was still Rae's father.

And people hadn't come to fear the name *Simon Kerrigan* for nothing.

Devon cursed in surprise as he was tackled off his feet. Before he could recover his senses, the knife was kicked out of his hand and Simon was kneeling on his back, pressing his face into the ground. There was a dull thud as the tatù-inhibiting anklet was broken off and thrown onto the grass, and a second later Simon had grabbed the bare skin on Devon's wrist.

"That's it..." his eyes closed with a nostalgic smile, "that's what I remember."

Devon's body jerked in surprise, and he grabbed not at his wrist but at his arm. At the skin where Rae knew his inked fox would be. He rolled out from underneath Simon a moment later, panting softly and clutching at his sleeve.

"What...what did you do to me?"

"Just evened up the playing field a little." Simon got to his feet as well, looking more animated and alive than Rae had ever seen him. "You don't mind a fair fight, do you, Devon?"

Devon's blank eyes flashed, and he raised his hands in a chilling invitation. "Come on, old man."

And just like that, they were off. Crashing into each other with unspeakable force. Both delivering and receiving a beating that neither man should have been able to survive. Around them, the rest of the school was still locked in a battle of their own—supernatural powers and fantastical abilities lighting up the sky with random bursts of color and screams. Everywhere Rae looked was absolute, unadulterated mayhem. But the two men were in a world all to themselves.

Each one battling to get to the girl they loved.

Each for very different reasons.

There was another burst of profanity, and they crashed to the ground once more. Rae's breathing grew weak and shallow as they wrestled there.

Each one trying to get the upper hand. Neither one able to do so.

Every attack Devon launched was countered. Every strike he made was anticipated. It was as if Simon was inside his mind, reading his every move before he'd thought to make it himself.

Their hands locked together again and again, and at one point Devon paused for a moment and stared up in astonished frustration, wondering if Simon might have access to other powers after all. The next second, he pulled back his fist for yet another punch that was almost instantaneously deflected.

It's because of Tristan, Rae suddenly understood. *Because he fights like his father.*

But no sooner had she thought it than a sudden tearing inside her chest made her cry out to the sky. Both men came to an instant pause, their heads snapping up to look at her. While Simon's face paled in rage, Devon's did so in horror. For a split second, that flicker of light was back in his eyes. Shining like a tiny beacon, just strong enough that she could see the man breaking inside.

"Rae...?" he called tentatively.

Then Simon smashed his body into the ground.

That flicker of recognition died as he tried to push back to standing, but by that time it was already too late. Simon had used his moment of distraction to catch him by the same arm that Julian had snapped just minutes earlier, twisting it up behind him at an impossible angle. Rae didn't see how it could possibly stay attached. A second scream ripped through the air. But this one wasn't hers. It was deeper and feral. Rae had never heard Devon scream like that in her entire life.

"Dad," she choked, "don't—"

But Simon was immune. He was kneeling atop Devon's back. Leaning so far down that his forehead touched the curled tips of Devon's unruly hair. "So, kid, you still going to get up and try to stab my daughter? Or have you snapped out of it already?"

He lifted the arm higher, and there was another scream.

"Let go," Devon panted, his face dangerously white. "Simon, let me—"

"Dad! Stop, please! He's not himself! It's not him," Rae panted, trying to catch her breath and be heard above the noise. "Get off him!"

"I want to hear you say it," Simon replied calmly, twisting Devon's head to the side so he could see him. "I want to see in your eyes that she's safe."

When those glassy, spellbound eyes did nothing but glare back at him, he twisted the arm higher still. Devon's head bowed in heart-wrenching agony, and he gasped softly against the ground. "Do it," he whispered.

Simon paused, then listened intently. "What was that?"

"Do it," Devon cringed into the grass, squeezing his eyes shut as tight as they would go, "so I can't hurt her anymore." Rae's heart broke and even Simon froze as tears slipped down Devon's face. "Simon, please..."

But whether Simon would have snapped off his arm or embraced him like a son, Rae would never know. Because it was at that moment that Rae realized she had bigger problems than her fiancée, or her father, or even the gaping wound in her chest.

Her mother had just arrived.

She saw the colors before she heard the screams. That was the way it always seemed to happen. An ironic warming of the sky before the devastation rained down from above.

They were a particular shade of blue—the flames of her mother's. Both terrifying and beautiful. The exact same shade as her eyes. A shade that Rae would never be able to forget for as long as she lived.

A wave of people went diving out of the way as Beth moved forward.

Sure enough, her entire body was engulfed in flames. An ice-blue storm cloud that streaked up behind her, like the wings of a devastating angel. Her chin jerked higher, and her eyes dilated almost black as they scanned the fleeing crowd. Searching. Planning.

Rae flailed her hand to get her mother's attention. Screaming with all her might to be heard above the crowd. But it was then that she saw something to make her blood run cold.

Her mother's eyes might have been blue.

But there was nothing left of her mother inside.

They were vacant. Just as vacant as Devon's, and Angel's, and Luke's. And they weren't scanning around for her daughter like she'd thought. They were focused on the people. All those hundreds of people, screaming as they raced for safety.

"MOM! NO!"

Simon followed her gaze in terror. Even Devon turned around as Beth slowly lifted her hands and pointed them in the direction of the crowd. A luminescent glow began building in the palms of her hands as Rae hitched herself up onto her shoulder with a soundless cry.

It should have been the end. The end of a great many things.

But fate, it seemed, had other plans.

As Rae looked on in breathless horror, a shadow blurred in the air between them. A shadow so swift and sure it was like it came from hell itself. In hindsight, she wasn't too far off the mark.

It was her father.

Simon released Devon and leapt forward, careening through the air towards Beth. In what felt like slow motion, he grabbed his estranged wife in his arms. Crushing her in an embrace so tight the flames themselves had no room to breathe. No room to expand and consume all those frozen, breathless people. To arch out over the sky and end their lives forever.

As the iridescent glow faded and died Beth gazed up with wide, tear-filled eyes.

"Simon?"

He leaned back with a soft smile, tinted with that same nostalgia as before. "I told you years ago, my love," he murmured softly, "I'd never let that beautiful fire of yours turn against you."

A sudden hush fell over the crowd, and the next thing Rae knew the strange collage of colors and abilities faded to a clear blue sky. As quickly as it had started, the spell had broken. The smoke began to drift away, but the crowd was rooted to the ground in shock.

All of them staring at Simon Kerrigan through brand new eyes.

For a full minute, nothing happened.

Then a young man stepped forward, no different from anyone else, bleeding profusely from the ear. He took one look at Simon and a sudden surge of wonder lit his face. "He...saved us."

After a split second, the same was echoed from every corner of the blood-stained grass. Bouncing back in a hundred different voices, each as astonished as the rest.

Rae lifted her eyes to her father, unable to believe what she'd just seen. "Daddy?" she whispered, then blacked out.

Chapter 3

Rae slowly woke to a world in transition.

The smoke had yet to clear. People had yet to lift themselves off the ground. She was still lying in the same puddle of blood she'd passed out in, only now there were two sets of cool hands pressed over her chest.

One belonged to Alicia—who was carefully mending the gaping wound that had been near her heart. The other belonged to Molly—who looked as if she would never dare let go.

They were soon joined by a third, as Beth, who had extracted herself from Simon, was looking slightly confused, and fell to the ground beside her daughter, pulling Rae up into her lap. "Oh, honey," she whispered and soothed, careful not to disturb Alicia's work as she stroked her daughter's blood-stained hair. "Honey, I'm so sorry. I tried to get to you. I tried."

Rae glanced around through half-closed eyes.

Simon was still standing exactly where Beth had left him. He seemed uncertain as to whether he would be permitted to join in. The eyes of the crowd were still on him, and as people began to slowly come back to life he seemed to brace himself where he stood, prepared for one ending or another.

Devon, on the other hand, was still in a complete daze. He slowly got to his feet, wincing in surprise, then cradling his shattered arm to his chest. His eyes widened as he stared at the grisly scene, but bit by bit he was beginning to put some things together.

"Jules?" he gasped, spotting his best friend lying behind him.

But Julian was already getting to his feet, albeit a little more broken than when he'd gone down. He was quickly aided by

Mitch Ford, who seemed on the verge of madness that he'd actually raised a hand against him. He fussed and coddled—as much as a massive, militaristic man was capable—but Julian waved both him and Devon off, limping towards Angel.

Undeterred, Devon rotated in slow motion and turned his eyes to his fiancée, still crumpled limply on the ground. "RAE!"

She tried to smile at him. Tried to show him it was okay, but she wasn't sure the smile made it to her lips.

He was in front of her the next second, but didn't seem to know what to do. It was like he didn't know what had happened, or how they'd gotten there. His eyes flickered down to the red puddle seeping slowly into the ground with the look of a bewildered child, before slowly, painfully slowly, making the journey back to his own hands.

His face lost all color, and for a moment it looked as though he'd been stabbed as well. "What have I done?"

It was strange that Rae even heard the words—as quiet as they'd been spoken, as noisy as the bloodied campus had suddenly become. But they rang out loud and clear. She could even hear his sporadic, shattered breathing as he robotically started backing away.

"Rae, I...I didn't mean to..."

He was quickly drowned out as a swarm of other people rushed forward, all of them in various states of disrepair. The second that Simon had caught Beth, whatever magic had been their undoing had suddenly been lifted. And while Rae's situation might have been the worst, it was by no means the only tragedy that happened on the grass that day.

Angel had rushed forward towards Julian, her eyes filled with tears, before suddenly remembering herself and doubling back to unfreeze Gabriel. Her brother had fallen forward, mid-run, and somersaulted back onto his feet just in time to see the new woman in his life save the old.

Commander Fodder looked as ashen as Rae had ever seen him. Somehow, even more so than when he'd gone with her on a journey into her father's deepest thoughts. A wide smear of blood was painted from his forehead to his chin, but at the moment his only thought was for his youngest son, who was still passed out cold at his feet.

"Luke," he murmured, dropping to his knees. "I'm so sorry, please...please come back to me. Luke—"

"Alicia," Rae muttered, shifting painfully higher into her mother's arms, "I'm fine. You fixed enough of it. Go and help him, okay?"

Alicia did a quick assessment before glancing behind her and taking off towards the men. It was clear that people would need to be triaged at this point. They would not be her only patients.

"I have your tatù, Alicia. Go." Rae swallowed, trying to appear more calm than she felt. Beside her, someone sniffed tragically.

"Rae, I don't know what happened." Molly gazed down at her with wide, watery eyes. "I saw Devon walking towards you... I knew something wasn't right. But when I tried to help, it was like I just couldn't. Something was stopping me... This voice inside my head. It told me to run, and I..." She bowed her head guiltily as tears dripped down her cheeks.

Rae reached up quickly and squeezed her hand. "Hey, it's not your fault. It was some power; there was nothing you could have done. Otherwise, you would have stopped." Her eyes flickered up to Devon without realizing it, willing herself to believe it to be true. "Otherwise, there would be no way you'd ever..." A hard lump rose in the back of her throat and she fell silent, turning her face in to her mother's jacket. It didn't help. Even with her eyes closed, she couldn't stop seeing it. No matter which way she turned, the same image kept creeping into her mind.

Devon walking towards her. Devon gazing down with a smile. Devon sliding the knife between her bones like she was made of tissue-paper. Staring indifferently down at her.

I have to kill you now.

A violent shudder ripped through her body, and she pushed Beth aside to throw up.

Devon was still standing exactly where she'd lost sight of him, a frozen statue in the middle of the crowd. He'd kept backing away from her until Simon had caught him by the shoulders and held him still. Devon didn't notice. His eyes were fixed on Rae. The exact spot where she'd been before all these people got in their way.

Staring as if he could still see her. Trembling as if he'd seen a ghost.

A pair of tears slipped down his face, and he whirled around to run—only to be caught again by Simon. Rae watched the two of them side by side, their profiles both strong, both looking lost in the confusion of what might have been.

Devon saw Simon this time, staring with wide-eyed disorientation as the man held him easily in place. Then, in a move that surprised them both Devon grabbed onto Simon's shirt, still silently crying, although he didn't seem to notice that either. "Please," it was almost hard to understand him, he was shaking so hard, "please...don't let me get near her. Don't let me hurt her again. I couldn't stop...I couldn't—"

Simon caught him in a sudden embrace. An embrace that was as much to restrain him as it was to calm him down. "It wasn't *you*, do you hear me? This wasn't your fault."

Devon just stood there in shock, bringing his hands up slowly behind Simon's back to stare at the blood on them. "But it was...I remember...I remember every—"

"That's enough," Simon said sternly, pulling back to look him up and down. "Rae needs you to be strong right now, do you understand? You need to be strong now, Devon."

Before he could answer, Simon pulled him back through the crowd, joining his estranged wife and daughter where they were huddled on the grass. The crowd was beginning to disperse now, like each one of them was prepared to drive away and never look back. At one point Louis Keene snatched up the microphone, assuring everyone that the Council would get to the bottom of this, that everything was going to be fine.

But it didn't sound like he believed it himself.

By the time he joined the rest of them, the entire group was gathered in a shaken circle—Rae and Beth still kneeling in the center. None of them spoke. None of them dared to meet the others' eyes. They simply stood.

Bleeding quietly. Trying to catch their breath. At a total loss as to what came next.

"We should all get back to the house in Kent," Commander Fodder said quietly. "It's so far off the grid that, until we know what we're dealing with, it's probably safer than the Abbey. It's certainly much safer than..." He caught himself before he could say the rest.

Than Guilder. Than the headquarters of the PC. Than this placed they'd called home.

When nobody made any attempt to answer him he turned to Devon, who was usually his best bet in terms of taking charge and coordinating logistics. But Devon just sank into a crouch, cupping his hand over his mouth, staring at Rae like she was dead already.

Already, huh? Quite the subliminal tag-on.

But deep down, Rae didn't see how it could *not* be true. Whatever had happened to them today wasn't like anything that had ever happened before. This wasn't like any enemy they had battled before. It didn't strike them from the outside. It attacked from within. Negating all strength and power. Using their deepest emotions and ties of loyalty against them.

How could they fight something like that? Something they couldn't hear. Something they couldn't touch or see. Something that divided, not united them.

It had attacked from within.

How were they going to battle this? Something they didn't even know was coming?

Chapter 4

The next moves became all about recovery.

The field was evacuated. Guilder was written off as a temporary bloodbath and emptied of all persons, students included, until further notification. The same was done with the tunnels underneath and the adjacent PC buildings connected to them. By the time the exodus was complete, not even the janitors remained.

In an impromptu gesture of inter-governmental spirit, the Abbey opened its doors. There was no limit to who or how many were welcome. The invitation was open-ended and immediate in effect, but in the end proved to be fruitless, albeit kind.

The reason was simple: no one felt safe.

If this kind of attack could happen on PC soil, then there was no reason to think that the Abbey would be any different. And if it could render the leaders of both governments helpless, even the invincible Rae Kerrigan and her band of heroic friends...then who could possibly protect them?

That being said, the super-gang wasn't feeling so heroic at the moment. And the invincible Rae Kerrigan had certainly seen better days.

"Stop moving around so much," Gabriel commanded, shoving Rae down with one hand as his other yanked up her shirt. "It's bad enough that I'm doing this in a moving car."

A searing pain shot through her body, landing somewhere in her teeth. While being vaguely aware that it was counterintuitive, she took a second to viciously slap at his hand. "Sorry," she hissed, glaring up with bloodshot eyes. "This must be so difficult for *you*."

An hour ago, Gabriel would have grinned slyly—as caustic as it might be. What now felt like forever ago, but was maybe a little over the sixty-minute mark, he would have been able to see the dark humor in things. But now? There was not a trace of levity on his face as he deliberately pressed her back down upon the leather seats and slipped onto the floor so he could better see what he was doing.

A cloud of warm breath tickled Rae's bare ribs, but the pain that followed overwhelmed all her other senses. Blinding her to the point where she, too, had room for no other emotion. "Freakin' A! Hurry up, Gabriel!"

He gritted his teeth but did as he was asked, holding out his hand as she quickly conjured and handed him a suturing kit. As the car swerved and darted through traffic he carefully threaded the needle, holding it above her skin with a steady hand.

It was the exact reason the two of them had ended up in this car together. Slipping away despite the horde of other people all tearing towards the parking lot, seeking refuge in other towns.

Gabriel's steady hands.

"You know," he glanced up for only a moment, "this would be a hell of a lot easier if you had taken some damn morphine in first place, like I told you—"

"No drugs," Rae interrupted, bracing herself between the armrest and the door as she spoke through gritted teeth. "This day's been warped enough without piling a heap of chemicals on top of it. Besides," she bravely stretched out her torso, providing him the easiest possible canvas, "what if whatever it was that happened before, happens again? I'll need to have my wits about me."

Gabriel's hands paused, and his green eyes burned into hers.

"If it happens again, I'll be right here." A bitter note of accusation leaked through the words, even as he strove to keep them neutral. "*I* won't let anything happen to you."

Rae's chest tightened, but she didn't respond. The last hour had been so convoluted and confusing, with such heavy emotion and blame flying in all directions, she truly had no way of knowing which way was up or down. And all that was *before* the massive blood loss...

"Okay," Gabriel's voice took on that practiced, reassuring tone it got whenever he slipped back into one of his Cromfield survival skills, "you ready?"

Rae shook her head. "No. I've changed my mind."

That coaxed a bit of a smile from him. His thumb stroked comfortingly against her skin before he leaned forward with a sudden look of concentration and began to work.

Pain beyond pain!

Rae jerked up her chin, and kept her eyes fixed on the ceiling. Somewhere, just beyond her vision, a tiny needle was flying back and forth, sealing shut whatever ravaged skin Alicia had been unable to mend before her services were urgently required elsewhere.

Under normal circumstances, Devon would be patching her up himself. At the very least he'd be sitting here beside her, holding her hand. Most likely shouting at Gabriel to work faster, or criticizing his technique. Making jokes or telling silly stories just to make her laugh. To distract her from the pain, and take her mind off whatever terrible thing had caused it in the first place.

...rather ironic.

Gabriel seemed to be thinking the same thing. And he seemed to be having a very, *very* difficult time not blaming Devon for what he'd done. His eyes flickered out the back window for a moment to the car behind them, before returning to her skin with a vicious glare.

"It's not his fault," Rae whispered, knowing his thoughts.

Gabriel's lips thinned to a hard line. "Hold still."

She did as she was told, flinching when the needle dug in once more. But she couldn't just let it rest. A part of her needed as many people to say it as possible. Maybe if they believed it was true, then she could start to believe it herself. "Gabriel, I'm serious—"

She broke off with a tortured cry at the same time that Gabriel cursed aloud and glared towards the front. The car swerved again, and they were tossed up against the side.

"*Really*, Angela?"

'Angela' only made an appearance in times of great stress. When all other stores of patience and calm were long since destroyed.

"What do you expect—it's chaos out here," Angel shot back, doing her best to cut along the side of what looked like a massive build-up in the center of the freeway. But she flashed them an apologetic grimace in the rearview mirror. "I'm sorry, guys, but we're not the only ones trying to get away from the pandemonium. How'd you ever survive going to school here, Rae..." her voice trailed off.

Rae ignored the last comment, too focused on the pain as she settled back down and on what Angel had said first. *Of course they weren't the only ones racing away. Because everyone else was just as freaked out as they were. They were all heading for the hills together. Frightened enough to scatter, rather than unite.*

"Rae." Gabriel gently pressed her back into the seat, and they started again. The pain was just as excruciating as ever and Rae closed her eyes, trying to focus on something steady.

"It wasn't Devon who did this," she tried again, more to herself at this point than to anyone else. "Blaming him isn't going to make it any better."

Gabriel sat quietly as he worked, and when he tied off the final knot he sighed. "I know that." He leaned forward and bit the string free, the edges of his lips sending little shivers up Rae's sides. "I couldn't break free to save you. He couldn't break free to save you, either. I can't blame him for failing to do what I wasn't able to do myself." He leaned back to examine his work, taping a bandage over it with another sigh. "But knowing that...doesn't help."

Rae sighed as well. *No, it doesn't.*

The solemn procession of cars that left the Kent mansion that morning could not have been a more different sight than the mad scramble that returned. From the second the doors opened it was as if their panic became a tangible fog, spilling out the open windows and quickly blanketing the sweeping lawns beyond. Coming right up to the doors of the house.

"Rae!" Molly screamed the second they were outside. She was outraged to have been placed in a separate car—but in the chaos of the moment there was little she could do. "Rae, are you alright? Did Gabriel get you patched up okay? You should have let Alicia do more before you sent her off to Luke—Luke was fine. I tried calling in the car. You're not picking up your—"

"Yeah, Molls. I'm fine." Rae caught her by the shoulders, well-familiar with the breathless rant. "I left my phone in the courtroom, I think." She brought a shaky hand up to her head, watching as the rest of the cars emptied out onto the drive. "I don't know, everything's a little—"

"Of course it is," Molly interrupted fiercely. "You got stabbed! *Again*!" Rae wished she would lower her voice but, if anything, pregnancy had only amped up her rather exuberant personality. "I thought we agreed, *no more stabbings*. Wasn't that the new slogan?!"

"Yeah...no more..." Rae trailed off faintly as Devon exited the car behind her.

Aside from that one, horrified moment when he'd fallen to the ground at her side, looking on in horror as Alicia slowly mended the wound, her beloved fiancé hadn't allowed himself to come within ten feet of her. It wasn't that he didn't want to. Rae could sense that. But it was more like he was literally unable. Not physically capable of risking her safety for even a second more. Even if it meant chaining himself to a tree somewhere until they figured out what was going on. Even if it meant taking a knife himself.

Sure enough, the second his boots hit the gravel he spun around in place—scanning the tiny crowd for her. They found each other quickly. But the second their eyes met he made no move to get closer. Instead, he did probably the last thing in the world Rae would have ever expected.

"Simon," he said bracingly, taking a step back.

It was called softly, but Rae could hear it all the way across the yard. She looked on in wonder as her father's head snapped up and followed her fiancé's gaze. A second later, Devon's jacket was secure in Simon's fist. Like it or not, the guy wasn't going anywhere.

"When did that happen?" she murmured quietly, speaking to no one in particular.

Molly, however, remained completely oblivious.

"Here, let me see—"

Before Rae could stop her, the tiny redhead had pulled up her shirt with little to no regard as to who might be watching, peeling back the side of the bandage so that she could examine Gabriel's work. Although the move was lost on the majority of the people limping past them inside, the sight was enough to stop both Devon and Simon dead in their tracks.

And to earn a vicious reprimand from Rae. "Would you stop that?!" she hissed, pulling it back down with a flush of guilt. Her eyes flickered up apologetically, but the damage was already done.

Simon tightened his grasp to an almost painful degree, his fingers clawing into the back of Devon's mangled shoulder without realizing what he was doing. Five small streams of blood leaked through the front of Devon's jacket, but despite how it must have felt the guy looked like he hardly noticed what was going on himself.

His eyes were locked on Rae. Riveted, without the slightest chance of moving. Staring at her ripped shirt as if he could still see the damage just underneath. The damage he'd done.

"Devon..." she called tentatively.

But he was in his own world. His head jerked once, as if he'd been slapped. Then he took a half-step back, further into Simon's restraining hands, looking a bit like he might be sick.

Molly's crimson ponytail whipped back and forth as she followed Rae's gaze, then she bowed her head with sudden understanding. "Sorry. I thought you guys had already talked."

Rae pulled in a deep breath to collect herself as her fiancé was whisked away. Presumably to be politely murdered somewhere by her estranged father. "Nope. No talking. In fact, if I know Devon he's never going to let himself get close enough to talk to me ever again."

Molly's face tightened sympathetically, but she tried to coax a smile. "Good thing you guys have that fox ink, then. You don't have to get close. The two of you are probably some of the only people on the planet who could carry on an entire conversation from separate buildings. No need to see each other at all."

Rae shot her an incredulous look, and she lifted a shaky thumb's up.

"See...problem solved."

The two of them shared a quick look before Rae's composure broke and she chuckled quietly. Sure. Problem solved. Why not? At this point, a protective space requirement between her and her fiancé was probably the least of her problems anyway. It was certainly more manageable than anything else going on. Leave it to Molly to put things in perspective.

Then chuckling turned into painful coughing, and she threw her arms around Molly's neck for support. "Just get me inside, you psycho. And try to remind me why we're friends."

As Molly launched into what sounded like an oddly pre-rehearsed list with gusto, Rae lifted her eyes to see Devon still watching her from across the drive. Simon had been distracted by Mr. Fodder, and while Molly was obliviously prattling on the two of them shared a private moment.

I'm sorry. The wind gently danced his hair across his forehead as he mouthed the words from the other side of the drive. *I'm so sorry.*

Rae's lips turned up in a sad smile. *I know.*

The next second, they lost sight of each other once more.

With the authoritative air of a pregnant woman used to getting what she wants, Molly elbowed a path straight for the coveted recliner in the living room. It was a chair which she had taken to using as something akin to a throne, but she graciously allowed Rae to use it instead. "Only until Alicia gets back and finishes healing you the rest of the way," she warned. "I don't want to set a precedent here of lax requirements. This thing has to be earned."

Rae flashed a weak grin and painfully leaned back against the cushions. "Noted. And you don't need to try to cheer me up, you know," she added more seriously, gazing up at the waves of tension straining her friend's face. "This isn't exactly new territory for me."

In hindsight, she almost wished she hadn't said it. For one of the first times she could remember every single shred of whimsy, spirit, and defensive humor melted from Molly's face. It left her looking years older than she was. Wilted, somehow. And chillingly grave. "Yeah, Rae. It actually is."

The defeated expression burned into Rae's mind, promising to haunt her for many nights to come. But before she could think of a single thing to say, a throat cleared in the center of the room.

"Are we all here now?" Commander Fodder did a silent tally. "Is this everyone?"

Such as it was.

Rae could think of no shortage of times when she'd gazed around the room, only to see her friends looking as though someone had tried to beat them to death. On most days, that was exactly what had ended up happening. The years had hardened them, and heaven knew they were no strangers to breaks, and cuts, and bruises. To be honest, it was a bit of a novelty now when they were all patched up and clean. It had long since become a joke that at least one of them had to have some blood on them.

But this... this was something different.

A long time ago, Rae's old mentor—the infamous Jennifer Jones—had told her something that she would never forget.

A punch hurts a hundred times worse when it comes from a friend.

Rae couldn't think of a better phrase to summarize the feeling in the room. These were no ordinary war wounds. They were looking at friendly fire. Every hurt, every tear, every drop of blood that had been spilled had been come at the hand of someone else sitting in that very room.

Father beating son.

Friend attacking friend.

Lover stabbing lover.

A belated chill ran through her shoulders and she hitched herself higher up onto the recliner, well-aware that she was leaving a crimson stain in the plush fabric. She needed a healing tatù of her own. One to fix this. Didn't she have one? If so, why wasn't it working?

"This is everyone," Beth answered him.

She was perched on the far sofa, sitting snugly in between Angel and Gabriel, a usually inseparable pair who suddenly couldn't seem to look at each other. It was a vantage point from which she could watch her ailing daughter and her estranged husband at the same time.

Fodder glanced around for a moment before nodding curtly. A second later he dropped his head, trying desperately to come up with something to say.

Rae almost felt sorry for him. He was clearly as out of sorts as the rest of them; he had been ever since he'd taken that not-so-merry trip with her down Simon's memory lane. And all that was before he and his youngest son had duked it out on the Guilder lawn. As it stood, he was keeping one hand on Luke at all times. Like he was terrified of what might happen were he to let him go. "Well...I think the first thing we need to do is figure out what happened," he began with his best attempt at practicality. "Clearly, we were all placed under some kind of—"

"We don't need to figure out what happened," Rae interrupted softly, "or who did it. I think we already know."

Even as she said the words, a familiar face flashed through her mind. The same face that had stared back at her amidst an angry mob the night of Thanksgiving. The same face Rae had invited as a guest into her home. The face of a girl who had walked calmly up to the podium just an hour earlier, and pressed a dagger into Devon's hand.

She swallowed hard. "Samantha."

Chapter 5

Half the room blanched in horror, while the other half blankly shook their heads. The name 'Samantha' was only known to those who had been living inside the mansion, and had absolutely no meaning whatsoever to the rest. Or, if anyone knew her, they didn't connect the dots.

"Samantha?" Beth questioningly cocked her head to the side, staring at her daughter as though worried the outburst might have less to do with fact and more to do with blood loss. "Who the heck is Samantha? Is Samantha an actual person?" she added in an undertone to Gabriel.

He didn't answer. He kept his eyes locked on Rae instead.

"Her?" His voice was clipped, dangerous. "The reporter?"

"Think about it..." Rae's eyes danced as she put the pieces together even as she spoke. "As a member of the press, she'd have access to places that other people wouldn't. But even so, the first time I met her was at a safe house after the kitchen exploded. She walked right into the room where I was being held just to talk to me. There's no way in hell she could have gotten in there without some supernatural help. A tatù."

Commander Fodder leaned forward in his chair. "You talked to a member of the press in the interrogation room? We don't have any record of that—"

"Maybe she just asked you to delete it." The more Rae thought about it, the more she was convinced. "Remember that guy we met at the Abbey, training against Cromfield? Benjamin Eeks?"

Gabriel flushed and leaned back in his chair. Benjamin Eeks had been responsible for inciting a fight between the Council and the Knights. A fight in which Gabriel had stopped the flow of blood to a man's heart just to prove a point. But Rae didn't mean it as any sort of jab. And for the first time, the others leaned forward with sudden interest.

Julian was particularly quick to get on the same page. "You think they have the same ink?"

Rae nodded her head, a grim smile on her lips. "Nothing more deadly than the power of persuasion..."

The coffee, she remembered. In the safe house, Samantha had told her to drink a cup of coffee. 'You'll need your strength for what's to come,' she'd said.

Rae hadn't been able to set the cup down.

"I'm sorry," Beth interrupted again. "Who are we talking about?"

"A little while ago, we gave an interview here at the house to a member of the Guilder Student Press," Rae explained to the adults in the room. "It was right after Simon was discovered at the house, during a time when we were getting a lot of bad publicity. Samantha made it sound like she wanted to write the other half of the story. Tell it from our side."

"But that's not what happened," Molly took over, her eyes locked on the carpet. "From the second she walked in here, all she wanted to do was talk about us. The group dynamic. Our history and our relationships."

"Makes perfect sense," Luke continued, "seeing as that's exactly what she used to play us all against each other today. Pitting me and my dad against each other, knowing the strength of that bond. Same thing with Angel and Gabriel. She used one to neutralize the other, weaponizing the last person in the world Gabriel would ever expect. It was the same thing with..." he trailed off, but his point was clear.

Without a doubt, Rae was the most dangerous person on the campus that day. The person most capable of stopping whatever it was that Samantha had planned. What better person to set against her than the man she loved? Who else stood a chance of even getting close?

"That voice in my head..." Molly murmured, her blue eyes glistening with unshed tears. "It told me to run."

Julian reached over and squeezed her hand. "Because you're pregnant. She knows you're pregnant."

Molly slowly brought a hand up to her belly while Commander Fodder pushed suddenly to his feet, too agitated to stay seated a second longer.

"So, what? You're telling me that all of this comes down to one demented girl?! A girl who decided to murder hundreds of tatùed people, but had enough of a conscience not to harm an expectant mother? How the hell is that possible?!"

"First of all," Louis Keene spoke for the first time, "I think we've long ago learned not to underestimate the extraordinary power of *one demented girl*." He cast Rae an indulgent look before turning back to Fodder. "And second, if this Samantha is in fact responsible for that happened at Guilder today, I don't think it was her intent to murder the people in the crowd."

Fodder and Keene usually got along very well. Rather splendidly, in fact. But the Commander was clearly hardly feeling like himself. The veins in his neck looked like they were in constant danger of rupturing, and even though he'd leapt to his feet he'd still managed to keep a protective hand on Luke, clamping down in an unbreakable death-grip upon his shoulder.

"*Really?*" His eyes narrowed with an impatient glare. "You think the fact that they all spontaneously decided to attack each other was just a coincidence, do you? Or perhaps you're simply taking comfort in the fact that no one actually *died*."

"That's part of it, yes," Keene replied calmly, glancing sympathetically at the connection between father and son. "No one died, and under the circumstances that fact alone seems incredibly unlikely. But my reasoning was a bit more personal than all that."

Fodder shook his head. "What are you—"

"The voice in *my* head," Keene interrupted. "It told me to stand perfectly still. To put my hands in my pockets and do absolutely nothing at all." His eyes flickered around the looks of confusion in the room before saying simply, "My tatù only kills. She didn't want me using it."

This sank in for a heavy moment, and then Rae cleared her throat. "Well, there's a simple way to find out. Jules," she swiveled around in her chair so the two of them were facing, "try to see what she's doing right now."

His face, still bleeding from his close encounter with Devon, lightened in surprise before he nodded quickly. "Oh! Right."

The room held its breath as the friends all angled towards him, waiting for his eyes to glass over to their customary white. He seemed to be waiting for it himself.

But it never happened.

"I can't," he finally murmured, strained with the effort of trying. His brow tightened in frustration as his hands gripped the edges of his chair. "Why the bloody—"

"Because she told you not to," Rae concluded. With the chilling clarity of hindsight, she remembered the exact moment it had happened. "By the front door, right after the interview. She told you not to go looking ahead to the future, that she wanted it to be a surprise." She remembered the strange look that had clouded his handsome face upon hearing the words. She hadn't thought anything of it at the time, just attributed it to the disastrous interview. "I'm sure it's the same way she walked right into the safe house to talk to me." Rae's mind raced back over the last few weeks, kicking herself for not seeing it sooner. "Now that I think about it, she's probably the one who incited the mob to come here the night of Thanksgiving."

"And the same one who made them leave," Gabriel interjected with a frown. "No offense, Rae, that was a great speech you gave, but they didn't come so far just to walk away. And it was more than that. They were... unnaturally persistent."

The room fell silent, and Rae realized with sudden clarity that he was right. She might have been on damage control since the moment she found her father at the factory, but it was Samantha who had been calling the shots. Every major event that happened since then, the girl had been there.

From the safe house, to the interview, to the night of the mob. At this point, Rae was even willing to bet that it had been Samantha who had somehow tipped off the press that she had been going to visit her father that day in prison. There was simply no one else who could have followed the convoluted route she took getting there. For all she knew the girl had hailed her down, asked her where she was going, then asked her to forget the whole thing.

"I just don't understand." She raised her voice in frustration, "First we're friends, and the next second she's telling us all to kill each other? What does the girl want?!"

"Me."

The entire room went quiet as everyone turned to stare at Simon.

He hadn't said a word during the entire conversation. Neither had Devon, on whom he kept a continual grasp. And even now, as the very fabric of their supernatural society was ripping apart at the seams, he seemed remarkably calm. Truth be told, he hardly looked surprised.

"That's what she told *me* to do. The voice in my head." The corners of his mouth twisted up into a humorless smile. "She told me to die."

There wasn't a single sound. Not a single breath.

Until...

"Then, why didn't you?"

Rae's eyes flew to Gabriel. Perhaps he hadn't meant it to sound like an accusation. Perhaps the soft malice in his voice was completely coincidental. To be honest, it was only the second thing he'd said to Simon since his resurrection, and he looked a bit surprised to hear it himself.

Simon met his eyes for only a moment before he turned deliberately to Rae. "I was wearing my anklet. I'm assuming it interfered with her tatù."

Rae nodded blankly, head still spinning from what she'd just heard. Then the implications of his words sank in, and her eyes flew down to his unshackled leg. "You aren't...your anklet..."

"I broke it off," Simon said quickly but calmly, his eyes flickering automatically to where both Fodder and Keene were realizing the problem at the same time. "I had to. In the time since it happened, I've done nothing to—"

"What the hell are you waiting for?" Angel demanded. For one of the first times ever, she was speaking directly to the Knights' commander. "*Do* something."

Fodder took a tentative step forward but Devon cringed back, leaning into Simon's grip on him like it was the only thing keeping him anchored to the planet.

"No! Don't!" He actually reached back and held Simon's jacket, angling himself protectively between the two men. "He had to break it off to get my tatù. Otherwise, he couldn't have..." His voice trailed hopelessly quiet as he lifted his eyes to Rae. "Otherwise, I would have..."

A look of supreme pity flickered across Fodder's face, and he paused where he stood. Both he and Keene shared a quick, confirmatory glance, before he sat back down with a sigh. "I suppose we can show a bit of restraint with Mr. Kerrigan, under the circumstances. And seeing as how you...you clearly have him, right Devon?"

Angel scoffed and turned away, but Rae instantly understood. At some point in the not too distant future, minutes of this entire meeting would be read by some clerk somewhere in an office room she would never see. A man tasked with determining the judiciary repercussions of everything happening that day in Kent. The morning might have been surrendered to chaos, but everything that happened in the afternoon would have to be strictly above board.

That being said, the notion that Devon *had* Simon was utterly ridiculous. Especially when it was so obvious that it was exactly the other way around.

"Uh...yeah." Devon flushed slightly, and dropped his eyes. "I have him."

Rae's heart broke a million times over, and she was aching to reach out to him.

But at that moment, Louis Keene leaned forward with a sudden frown. "Restraint must also be shown given the enormous debt of gratitude the tatùed world owes to Mr. Kerrigan for his actions today." His face paled a bit as he remembered. "Simon, I truly don't know what would have happened if you hadn't done what you did."

This time, it was Beth who dropped her eyes. Despite the fact that she had been just seconds away from passing out, Rae remembered the moment perfectly. How her mother had raised her hands, dripping with lethal fire, and aimed them at the crowd. How her father had swooped in at the last second and caught her in a fierce embrace. One strong enough to put out the flames. One strong enough to save the life of every single person who had come out to see him hang.

Keene pushed to his feet, crossing the room to extend his hand. "On behalf of all of us... I thank you."

Simon hesitated a moment as the room froze still. Then, with the hint of a smile, he reached out carefully and shook the hand of the Vice President of the Privy Council.

It was a tense moment considering the fact that, if Simon were to absorb Keene's power, it was unlikely that even Rae could put him down in time. But there was something strangely natural about it as well. As if Simon hadn't just come onto their side. As if there was a chance that he had already been there for quite some time.

"It was my pleasure."

It was those four words that ended the meeting.

Gabriel's eyes locked upon their frozen handshake for no more than a second before he got to his feet and swept from the room. Rae finally succumbed to the pain surrounding her roadside stitches and quickly conjured herself a vial of morphine. And at that same moment, the doorbell rang. Alicia was back from making her battlefield rounds, ready to fix up any lingering injuries the gang might have suffered before collapsing for the night in utter exhaustion.

The impromptu meeting silently dispersed as, one by one, people met with the doctor and vanished off to their separate corners of the house.

First up was Molly, much to everyone's great insistence, although she was one of the few people who hadn't actually come under attack. But Rae was right after. She sat perfectly still as Alicia calmly rolled up her shirt and peeled back the bandage to examine the hasty patch-job.

"You're certainly not flinching," she noted, frowning slightly as she leaned forward to get a better look. "Are you already on some pain meds?"

"Morphine," Rae breathed, leaning back in utter relief. "And not a second too soon."

"Yeah, I'll bet." Her cool fingers expertly prodded the edges of the wound, making careful note of the stitching. "Gabriel did this?" She sounded impressed.

Rae glanced down, and under the influence of the morphine she couldn't help but grin. "Yep. In a moving car, too." Her eyes twinkled mischievously as the tops of Alicia's cheeks blushed pink. "Note to self: the guy's good with his hands."

Alicia blushed even deeper and refused to meet her gaze.

Undeterred, and feeling the effects of the narcotics more with each passing second, Rae leaned forward with a loud whisper. "That was a sex joke—"

"Yeah, I got it. Thank you...for that." Alicia shook her head with a rueful grin, and shoved Rae down a little harder than necessary as her fingers lit up with their healing glow. "If this weren't quite so deep, I'd just leave you to suffer... note to self."

Rae chuckled, but the grin faded the longer she stared down at the light. Already, the edges of her skin were magically sealing themselves back together as the row of sutures fell away. "...it's really that deep?"

Alicia sobered in an instant, and gave her a sympathetic squeeze. "Yeah, it is. But I guess, in a weird way, it shows how much Devon loves you, right?"

Rae blanked and stared back at her, sure she must have misheard. "How the heck do you figure that?"

The last of the stitches fell away, revealing a patch of unblemished porcelain skin, and Alicia pushed back up to her feet. "This is *Devon* we're talking about. *Devon Wardell*. If he was handed a knife and told to kill you...you think he doesn't know how to do that?" Her lips turned up in a wry smile as she headed up the stairs to tend to the rest of them. "You think he just missed?"

Rae's lips parted in surprise as the simple truth settled over her. She hadn't even considered it. In the heat of the moment, it was impossible to consider it. But if there was one thing she could say for certain about her superhero fiancé, it was this...

Devon didn't miss.

In a flash, she was on her feet. The realization propelled her forward, filling her with a sudden sense of purpose as she swept out of the living room and set off to find him.

As desperate as he was to keep a safe distance between them, she was just as desperate to be in his arms. To tell him that he didn't fail her, that there was nothing to forgive. That, if anything, his unconditional love had actually saved her life. Breaking through a supernatural grip so powerful, it was a testament to the bond between them that she was even alive.

And speak of the devil...

"Devon!"

Rae rounded the corner to see both him and Simon on their way outside. The two of them paused by the front door as she hurried to catch up. She skidded to a stop, and for a split second it was all she could do to stare.

The sight of it was still utterly bizarre. Her fiancé and her infamous resurrected father standing side by side in the doorway. Out for a casual stroll on a crisp November afternoon.

Not that Simon knew she and Devon were together, of course. But at this point, Rae didn't see how he could have possibly not figured it out. As if that almost kiss at her childhood home and Luke's hastily halted speech wasn't enough, Devon has basically asked that Simon rip off his arm just a few hours earlier, all to prevent him from harming one more hair on Rae's head.

Sure enough, Simon cast a quick look between them before stepping forward with a smile. "You're looking better." Unable to mask his extreme relief, he reached forward and gave her arm a tentative squeeze, careful to avoid her skin. "Finally, a bit of color to your face."

A series of chills ran down Rae's arm, cascading out from the point of contact. It was the first time she could remember her father touching her since she was six years old.

"Alicia healed you?" Devon asked quickly, scanning her shirt as if he could still see through it to the damage below. "There weren't any...complications? You're okay?"

"I'm okay." Rae emphasized each word carefully, willing him to meet her eyes. "As good as new, actually. It's like it never happened."

If only Devon could see it the same way.

A look of gut-wrenching remorse flickered through his bright eyes before he dropped his gaze to the floor, nodding quickly even as he edged to the door. "Well, that's...Rae, I..." He pulled in a quick breath, and pulled open the door. "I think it's probably best if I—"

"Can I talk to you for a minute?" she interrupted. Over the years, she had been victim of enough of Devon's 'protect her from unseen danger' schemes to swiftly nip this one in the bud. He would not walk away. She would not allow it.

A look of fear flashed across his face, and he moved instinctively closer to Simon. As if the man was the only thing standing between him and the end of the world. "Uh...of course. Simon, do you mind?"

Rae lifted her eyebrows as her father froze uncertainly between them. "You're asking my father to chaperone?" She tried to lighten the mood.

Devon missed the joke. "I'm asking your father to make sure I don't kill you. Yeah."

The air between them suddenly chilled and Rae took a step forward, lowering her voice self-consciously as Simon discreetly looked away. "Why are you acting like you're mad at me?"

Devon's mouth fell open in surprise even as he took a step back, reestablishing the distance between them. "Like I'm...Rae—are you kidding? Of course I'm not *mad* at you; in what dimension would that possibly make sense?"

"Then why—"

"Why the hell are you acting like it's safe for us to be around each other?" he interrupted. "Like I don't pose some kind of threat?"

Rae caught her breath, but forced her voice to remain calm. "It's *over*, Devon. The whole thing is—"

"Stop." He shook his head. "You know better than that."

It was only then that Rae realized his arm was still hanging on by a thread, shaking with involuntary spasms as his jacket dripped blood all over the floor. Knowing him like she did, it was easy to imagine him refusing to be healed. Bearing the pain like a punishment.

A punishment he didn't deserve.

"You *didn't* kill me." By now, Rae was no longer concerned with her father's presence. They were past those kinds of embarrassments now. Her only goal was to make Devon understand. "She whispered it right in your ear, and you still made yourself miss—"

"Once." His face paled to a dangerous shade of white. "I missed once. I have no idea what would happen if I tried it again."

Simon's eyes flickered over them, but he pursed his lips and said nothing.

"But it's *done*, Devon," Rae repeated with a hint of frustration. "You and everyone else have completely snapped back to normal—"

"It's not *done*," he countered. "Not by a long shot."

In a wave of frustration, he actual forgot about his self-imposed safety protocols and took a step towards her, leaving Simon standing by the door.

"Don't you get it? I have no idea what exactly she told me to do. What if she said to try again later? What if I'm triggered by a word? What if this thing never really turns off and I—"

"That's not going to happen," Rae said firmly, stepping forward until they were standing toe to toe. Her fingers tentatively stretched towards his, as they stared into each other's eyes. "This is you and me. It's going to take more than a sixteen-year-old psychopath to tear us apart."

Well, if Simon didn't know before, he certainly knew now.

Devon pulled in a shuddering breath, and without seeming to think about it his fingers laced with hers, circling gently around the one that was supposed to be wearing her ring. "I just can't...I can't take that risk." His head snapped up with sudden illumination. "Maybe it would be different if Kraigan took my power. Just until we catch the little—"

"Are you kidding me?" Rae snapped. "You want my immortality to come back?"

Again, Simon lifted his eyebrows, but remained silent.

"Actually...yeah." For the first time, Devon's lips twitched up in a hint of a smile. "That sounds kind of perfect right about now."

Rae flashed him a rueful grin and shook her head. "Well, that's too bad. Because I have no intention of living forever, and you—you brooding bastard—are going to need your powers."

He opened his mouth to protest, but she lifted a silencing finger to his lips.

"You're right about one thing, Dev—this *is* just starting. And that means that we're going to need everyone at the top of their game if we want to get ahead of it." She squeezed his hand before pulling back to look seriously into his eyes. "That means you're going to have to accept that you had no control over what happened, forgive yourself, and move on. I need you with me, Wardell. Not sulking powerless in the shadows."

Again, a hint of that sparkling smile tugged at the corners of his lips. "...I don't sulk."

She threw back her head. "You are the biggest freakin' sulker I know."

At this point, Simon seemed to think it wise to excuse himself. "In that case, if you won't be needing my services," he backed towards the stairs with a little smile, "I think I'm going to track down that doctor and see if she can help me with a couple of these broken ribs." He caught the look on Devon's face, and held up his hands. "It's no problem. We all go nuts and break each other in half every now and again..." With that bit of way too soon humor, he vanished upstairs to find Alicia.

Devon, in the meantime, tightly wrapped his good arm around Rae's back. "Sweetheart, I'm so *so* sorry. I can't even begin to—"

She silenced him with a kiss. "I know."

They kissed again, and then she pulled back with a smile.

"And it's not me you have to say it to." Taking him firmly by the hand, she headed up the stairs to fix his arm as well. "You only stabbed me. You should see what you did to Julian..."

Chapter 6

"I'm just saying, honey, you were just *stabbed*." Beth flitted helplessly in front of her daughter down the stairs, wringing her hands more desperately with every step. "Don't you want to maybe give yourself a day to recover?"

Rae hastily stuffed her arms into her jacket, pausing only a moment to mournfully note the giant blood-stained hole in her favorite sweater.

"I told you, Mom, I'm fine." She nodded a silent greeting to Molly, who was already by the door, lacing up a pair of tall leather boots. "Alicia healed me. I'm as good as new."

"*Almost*," Molly muttered, eyeing her clothes critically. "It's like Devon didn't realize that sweater was a gift. From *Prada*."

Rae rolled her eyes. "Oh, I'm sure he wouldn't have stabbed me then."

"Too soon, guys," Luke muttered as he breezed into the room, having narrowly escaped the restraining hands of his father. "Way too soon."

"What?" There was a swish of air as Angel slid down the banister to join them. "I think it's good the guy starts taking responsibility for his actions."

Molly nodded soundly while Rae shot Angel a sarcastic look.

"Is that right? Just like you freezing Gabriel back at Guilder?"

Angel paused only for a second before shrugging it off in a way unique to her and her endearingly sociopathic brother. "I was under a spell."

"*So was Devon.*"

"Rae, honey, seriously," Beth tried again, discreetly angling herself in front of the door. "I think the lot of you are jumping the gun here. Why don't you reassess in the morning? After having gotten a good night's rest."

Rae shook her head, stepping into pair of boots before realizing they belonged to Julian. "No can do, Mom. We've got a lead. We've got to chase it down."

"Did I hear my name?"

Everyone looked up at the same time to see Devon and Julian slowly descending the stairs. The two of them had just had a miniature heart-to-heart—after one tried to strangle the other, a brief apology seemed socially appropriate—and were already geared up and ready to get on with the mission.

"Yeah." Angel peered up speculatively. Julian and Devon may have been as inseparable as two people could be, but she was slightly less inclined to forgive the man who had almost murdered her boyfriend. "Molly and I were just saying how it was high time that you—"

"That you get down here," Rae interjected quickly. "It's time to go."

Angel rolled her eyes and returned to her scarf, while Devon nodded and began tossing people their cell phones, one by one.

Julian secured his long hair into a ponytail, and nodded to Rae. "You want me to go? Then I need my shoes."

She glanced down and blushed, quickly locating her own. "Oh, sorry."

By now, Beth had been joined by both Simon and Commander Fodder. Each of them was watching the children suit up with varying looks of disapproval. All except Simon, of course. He was watching with a faint twinkle in his eye, an almost-nostalgic smile dancing around his lips.

"I don't know what cars we're going to take," Gabriel said as he breezed into the room; his hand shot up automatically as Devon tossed over his phone. "As long as we bring Kerrigan along, all of them are at risk of either getting ticketed or towed."

The rest of them chuckled under their breath, while Rae bristled defensively.

"When is that going to *stop* being funny?" she demanded.

Julian, the most recent victim of her vehicular sabotage, shot her a cool glare. "When you *stop* losing our cars."

She wisely decided to let it go.

"*Rae!*" Beth exclaimed again, finally summoning her full attention. "I want you to take this more seriously. You all just went through a *trauma*." She stared around at their blank faces. "Why the hell am I the only one who seems to grasp this concept?!"

"They're super-agents, Beth. It's their job, you know that," Simon interjected with a smile. "I, for one, think it's great that they're jumping back in the saddle so soon."

Beth's eyes flashed with a hint of her deadly fire. "Well, fortunately, no one asked you." She turned back to the kids. "I don't care if you've all technically been healed; there's more to recovery than just the physical. There are psychological ramifications to days like this. Scars that can't just be ignored." When no one said a word, she spun around in frustration. "Anthony, back me up here!"

It was always strange to hear the Commander referred to by his first name. Most of the time, Rae simply assumed that he didn't have one. Kind of like how it used to be with Carter.

He stepped forward with a frown, arms folded firmly across his chest. "I agree with Beth. It's far too soon for you to be gearing up for something like this." His eyes settled upon Luke, as if he was considering making him some sort of leash. "If we were back at the Abbey, I would order you all under medical supervision for at least twenty-four hours. Or, better yet, I'd send out a different team altogether to carry out such a task."

"And that's why the Knights will always come in second place," Devon murmured with a sly grin. He and Julian shared a silent fist pound before Luke stepped in between.

"You want to say that a little louder, Wardell?" He raised his eyebrows with a friendly, yet competitive, grin. "Maybe you and I can settle it outside."

"I'd place money on that," Julian said smugly.

"Yeah?" Molly blew him a shower of sparks. "So would I."

"It'd be an interesting fight," Gabriel murmured, generally ignoring the rest of the banter as he hastened to find all his clothes. "That's for sure."

Angel giggled. "Yeah, until Devon whipped out a knife and stabbed him."

The room went quiet. Dead quiet.

The adults blanched. Devon looked depressingly deflated. And as the others graciously averted their eyes, Angel gazed up questioningly at Julian.

"Was that too soon again?"

He put an arm around her, and silently steered her out the door.

As the others were quick to follow, Rae glanced at Devon. "It's fine, Dev. It's just... the way we roll, right? We joke around about stuff to deal with it."

"I know." He shot her an apologetic smile. "I'm sorry, again." He leaned over and kissed her forehead. "I've never been sorrier for anything I've ever done." He stepped outside and Rae went to follow.

She paused and then doubled back and took her mother by the hands. "Mom, it's not like we can take a day off, you know that. If there's trouble out there, then it's our job to find it. It's what we signed up for."

Beth's eyes watered as they automatically traced over the exact spot that the knife had pierced Rae's clothes. "Then at least let me come with you. Watch your back."

Rae pressed her lips tight, refusing to let the smile escape. On almost any other day, she'd bend over backwards to take her mother up on the offer. Having Beth Kerrigan watching your back was as close as you could possibly get to a guarantee. But that was most days. Today was a little different.

Today, the adults were feeling a little overprotective. And if the gang was going to have any chance at all of stopping Samantha, they needed to get back into their usual stride.

"I need you to stay here in case she comes back. She's already been here once; there's no telling what might happen if she decides to do it again." Rae glanced behind to where both her father and the Commander were standing side by side. Both impossibly powerful. Both impossibly different. "Besides," she lowered her voice to a loud whisper, "you need to keep an eye on these two. You know men." She rolled her eyes. "Delicate little flowers."

Beth shot her a sarcastic smile, and took a step back. "I'll do my best."

Rae grinned and hurried out after her friends, feeling oddly normal as she glanced back at her mother, and her father, and the leader of a secret organization of superhuman spies. All standing framed in the doorway of her enormous country estate. "I'm on my cell!" she called, spotting a tuft of crimson hair and sliding into the nearest car next to Molly. "Don't wait up!"

"Unless you want to order some dinner, that is!" Molly called through the window. "There are some take-out menus in the drawer by the fridge, and we all like Italian!"

The boys were quick to echo these sentiments, each adding their favorites. It wasn't until actual flames began dripping from Beth's hands that they had the sense to quiet down.

The trio of cars revved to life and whipped around the gravel driveway, blasting loud music from the windows as they shot off to the last place in the world that any of them wanted to see again.

Guilder.

By the time Rae and the gang got back to the scene of the crime, the sun was already setting behind the tall trees. A full moon was shining high in the sky above them, casting long shadows down through the branches and creating a strangely familiar feeling of adolescent criminality to the entire endeavor.

It hadn't been that long ago that Rae and Molly, as well as Julian and Devon, had been trying to sneak out of this campus instead of trying to sneak in. Lowering themselves down from their dorm-room windows high in the tall, stone towers. Slipping over the wide emerald lawns, as soft as spirits. When the necessity arose, even turning into the occasional bird.

You name it, they had done it. Their names were forever engraved in the sacred halls of the school. Living on as legends far after they had graduated and left such things behind them.

That being said, the lot of them still jumped like a group of frightened school children when they heard an oh-so-familiar voice...

"*Rae Kerrigan!*"

Molly jumped into Rae's arms with a shriek as all four of the boys leapt protectively in front of them. Trained to expect the worst Gabriel's arm shot up at the ready, pointing a loaded gun.

Only Angel remained immune, engrossed in a silent game on her phone.

"Madame...Madame Elpis?" Rae smacked down Gabriel's hand as she ventured cautiously forward. "Is that you?"

It was a fair question. Never before had the friends seen the poor woman so thoroughly undone. Her skin was a sallow kind of pale, and her wiry fingers trembled with every halting breath. Her clothes were torn and hung on her skeletal frame. Even her graying hair, always tied back in the strictest of buns, was hanging ragged down to her shoulders.

The woman made a strange, choking sound before lifting a quivering finger.

"Kerrigan! Skye! This is your final warning!" Her eyes bulged frightfully as her voice rose in panic. "If I catch you out after curfew one more time, it'll be a permanent mark on your record!"

Molly and Rae shared a bewildered glance as the rest of them stared in shock. Julian's eyes flashed in and out of the present. Angel slowly lowered her phone.

"Madame Elpis," Molly spoke carefully, like she was worried about setting her off, "Rae and I have been out of school for a while now. We graduated over a year ago."

Elpis' head jerked back and forth, as though seeing some kind of tennis match the others could not. When she realized Molly had spoken, her eyes—eyes so infamously sharp that they never missed a thing—darted back to the group in shock. Like she was seeing them for the first time.

"Children, what are you doing here?!" She frantically waved her hands towards the dorms, trying to shepherd them all inside. "Get to bed at once! It's not safe!"

...not safe?

Rae and Devon locked eyes for a split second before he took a step forward. "Madame Elpis," he began softly, "have you been on campus all day?"

If it was possible, her hands shook even harder. Her eyes darted wildly out to the bloody field next to Lawrence Hall, but she didn't say a thing.

At this point, Rae wasn't sure if she was even capable.

Oh, you poor thing...

When a person lived on campus, they were oftentimes overlooked when making a final tally. It wasn't at all hard to imagine how, when everyone else sprinted for their cars to escape, she was left behind. Lost in all the chaos. Unheard over the deafening clamor. Left alone in the unending silence that followed.

A look of extreme pity flashed across Devon's face as he silently removed his jacket and draped it over her shoulders. It was near freezing outside, but the woman was wearing nothing but a dress.

At the same time, Julian stepped forward and took her by the hand with a reassuring smile. "Actually, I think you're right. We should probably be getting inside." His voice took on a soothing, almost hypnotic quality. One that never failed to hit its mark. With careful nonchalance, he spun her around so she was no longer looking at the bloody field. Angled so she was looking back towards the safety of the school instead. "Can you walk me back to Joist?"

And that is why I love Julian Decker.

Devon gave him a tiny nod as Madame Elpis gazed up at him with wide, unblinking eyes. At first, Rae was worried that she didn't even understand the question. But a second later her head jerked up and down in a quick nod, and they started walking.

As they neared the door to the boys' dormitory, he slipped a comforting arm around her bony shoulders. By the time they stepped inside, she was openly sobbing into his shirt.

The friends were quiet, staring after them a long time after they'd gone. It wasn't until Molly started shivering in the chilly night, that Devon cleared his throat. "We should get inside ourselves. Jules knows the plan. He'll meet us in the library."

Rae and the others nodded and quickly set out across the lawn. But even as they hurried past the dorms and into the main building of the school she couldn't help but glance back, fixing her eyes on the door to Joist Hall.

Her mother was right. Not all damage could be seen on the surface. Some scars went a lot deeper than that. Some scars could never hope to fade.

She would never be so flippant again. They would give this day its due.

Before they did, they still had to find the girl responsible for all this mess.

But before that, they had to make sure a day like this would never happen again.

Chapter 7

Two hours later, they had yet to make any progress.

The seven of them were sprawled out in various states around the Scriptorium library, having already extracted all the administrative files from the office just inside and spread them out on the long table. Rae figured having superpowers would come in handy at a time like this, but try as they might, not one of them had been able to find a single word or shred of evidence on Samantha.

"I don't know what to tell you, Rae." Devon stretched his recently healed arm above his head with a muffled sigh. "If she was really a student here at Guilder, we'd have found her admissions form in one of these files."

Rae dropped the box of papers she'd been carrying onto the table in frustration. "But she told me she worked for the Guilder Student Press. It's such a minor detail to add, considering she could have just made me tell her anything she wanted to know. Why would she make up something like that?"

"I don't know, but she did." Molly waved half a dozen newspapers in the air, dangling her legs down from the top of a nearby bookshelf. "I've looked through issues and mock-ups for the last seven months. There's not a single mention of a Samantha Neilson anywhere."

As Rae dropped her head to the table, Julian slid a fresh cup of coffee her way.

"You know, there's also the possibility she said it because she didn't *want* to make you tell her anything she wanted to know." His face softened thoughtfully. "That she wanted it to be your choice."

For the first time, Rae considered this. Her gut reaction was that it was a stupid idea—the girl clearly had no problem pulling the strings of everyone around her. Why would she want to hear Rae frame the words herself instead of just extracting them with her power?

Except, the longer she thought about it the more she started thinking that Julian might be right.

She remembered the hungry way Samantha had asked after her father. *Simon Kerrigan.* The adoring gleam in her eyes when she talked about Rae and her friends. That shell-shocked look of awe the first time she had met them in person. It was a look that was quick to fade once they started talking about Simon. Once she realized that they didn't see things as black and white as she did.

"She idolized us," Rae murmured, "and absolutely hated my dad."

There was a slight pause before Gabriel spoke softly from the corner. "Then talking with you couldn't have been easy that day at the house."

Rae's mind flashed back as, once again, she considered. He was right. In fact, the more she thought about it the timeline made perfect sense.

Samantha had been dying to talk to her back at the safe house, dying to hear all about how Rae and her band of super friends had blown up their own mansion to stop the evil Simon Kerrigan once and for all.

...until she learned that wasn't exactly what happened.

After that, she came back with a mob.

Then she had been dying to let Rae and the gang explain themselves. To give them a chance to justify what had happened. But at the same time, she'd been arming herself as well. Teaching herself the ins and outs of their relationships. Figuring out their dynamic in case the answers they gave weren't the ones she wanted to hear.

They weren't. But when Rae promised to testify against him, everything changed.

She remembered the way Samantha's pen had hovered over the paper. The way her eyes dilated with absolute focus as she demanded that Rae say it again. Confirm it was true.

Rae had done exactly that. And nothing else went wrong. There was a temporary truce.

But then came the day of the trial.

Rae hadn't seen Samantha until the very end, but she was sure that she'd been there the whole time. Listening. Watching. Waiting to see what would happen.

In her eyes, it must have looked like everything was going according to plan. Rae travelled back into her father's past. Confirmed that everything the witnesses had said about him was absolutely true. Declared that he was guilty beyond any shred of doubt.

But then, that age old question came back to bite them all in the ass.

Death, or life in prison?

Rae advocated for life. A life barred from the rest of society. A life spent caged where he could sit and forever reflect upon the horrors of what he'd done. But it was life nonetheless.

After that?

...They all knew what happened after that.

"So, it was never about us. It was always about my dad."

Both Gabriel and Angel looked cold and unmoved, but graciously kept their thoughts to themselves. The rest of them, however, were piecing things together with that same dawning realization that Rae was feeling.

"I guess that makes sense," Devon finally admitted, automatically muting his phone as it buzzed against his hip. "Even if she is a little young to have so much of a personal vendetta. What doesn't make sense is why we can't seem to find her in any of these files." He shoved the pile in front of him, toppling it over in frustration. "She obviously has ink, and she's the right age. She's not a Knight, so why the hell wouldn't she be at Guilder?"

"Maybe because she has too much ink."

The group turned as one to look at Luke. He was propped up against the wall, a book in his lap and his feet on the table. He hadn't said much since their little run-in with Madame Elpis outside, but that was his habit. When Luke spoke, he liked to make it count.

"You guys remember Benjamin Eeks? The guy with the power of persuasion back at the Abbey?" The others nodded, and Luke continued carefully. "I've known Ben my entire life. We grew up training together. His ink was strong, but there was a breaking point to it as well. As long as you focused with complete attention—there was a way to beat it. Not like this girl." A belated shudder ran through his shoulders.

A shudder that all of them shared.

Luke continued, "But Samantha's ink is different in other ways, too. Training at the Abbey is a lot like the training you guys did back at the Oratory. We all spar against each other. Ben used his power on me many, many times." He closed the book and leaned forward. "In all those times, I never—*not once*—heard his voice inside my head."

A profound silence followed this remark. A silence that seemed to grow all the heavier the longer they let it stay.

"So, you're saying she's a hybrid." By now, Rae didn't even phrase it as a question. They all knew it was true.

It explained why she wasn't at Guilder, why she'd stayed off the supernatural radar. It also explained why not a single person on campus that day was able to resist her deadly charms.

The power of persuasion was bad enough when it was whispered in your ear. Fighting off a voice that was inside your mind—that was a different thing entirely.

And the fact that they were dealing with a dangerously disgruntled *kid*...?

Rae slowly pushed her chair away from the table, her eyes locked on the piles of books. "Things just got a whole lot more complicated."

The others murmured their agreement, but Angel tossed back her long hair.

"Complicated, yes. But not unclear." Her sapphire eyes flashed as she turned to her brother, who was already nodding in the corner. "We still know what we have to do."

"We have to find her," Gabriel finished. "She must be stopped."

Rae stifled a sigh as she looked at them.

Forever at the ready. Eyes dilated and focused. Hands always a second away from reaching for the weapons stashed inside their coats.

...and Cromfield's influence lives on.

Molly apparently thought so, too, although she was much more vocal with her opinion. "I'm sorry if the rest of us need a minute." She glared, visibly chafing at the idea of tracking down a sixteen-year-old girl. "I forgot that this must be old hat for you."

Angel cocked her head to the side. "Old hat?"

"You know...tracking down hybrids. Putting them in the ground."

"*Molly*," Julian chided sharply.

"What?" She looked around indignantly. "I'm just saying what we're all thinking. This girl is just a freaking kid. A kid with immense power and a giant chip on her shoulder. But I mean, look at the people right here in this room! Are any of us in a position to hold that against her?"

"We are when she tries to make us kill the people we love," Devon murmured.

"She's *sixteen*, Devon."

"Sixteen and impossibly dangerous," Gabriel replied unfeelingly. "If you're finding yourself a bit squeamish, what with the baby, then rest assured. The rest of us will do what has to be done."

"*Gabriel*," Julian chided just as sharply.

Molly slowly got to her feet, her fingers crackling with pent-up energy and sparks. "You're really going to bring my unborn child into this, Alden?" Her voice was surprisingly flat as she stared him down. "You really think that's a good idea?"

"Guys! Come on!" Julian got to his feet as well, standing in between them. His eyes flashed intermittently white, checking to see how far the fight would go. "This isn't helping."

"Tell *him* that," Molly hissed.

"I just *did*, Skye. Now sit down."

"Jules is right." Rae slapped her hands on the table, raising her voice to be heard above the clamor. "If there's one thing we learned today, it's that we're going to have to stick together if we want to have any chance of beating this thing. We're stronger united, weaker apart."

Angel snorted, whipping out her phone. "I think I read that on a t-shirt somewhere—"

"Would you put that damn thing away!"

A bolt of electricity fired through the air, zapping the mobile into oblivion.

"HEY!"

All eyes turned at once to Molly, but she lifted her hands innocently above her head.

It was Rae who lowered her smoking fingers back to her side, fixing Angel in a steady glare. "We don't have time for your indifference or your games." She was on her feet, depressingly aware that little lines were forming throughout the room. Spider-webbing and splintering the friends onto different sides. Fracturing them in ways she was terrified would splinter them apart forever. "This is exactly what Samantha wants. It's exactly why she came to the house that day. To find out our allegiances. Bonds to be broken, things that can divide." Her eyes flashed as they locked onto each one of her friends in turn. "We *cannot* let that happen."

The room abruptly fell into a tense silence. One which Rae was sure no one really knew how to break. It wasn't often that collective stress gave way to these sorts of fractures. They had simply been through too much together to be derailed by anything now.

Fortunately, the moment resolved itself.

Rae perked her head up at the same time as Devon—both hearing things that the others couldn't. The sound of a dozen cars pulling into the Guilder lot. The sound of footsteps clamoring their way, soon accompanied by the sound of voices.

"What is it?" Gabriel asked quietly. "What's going on?"

The others had long ago learned to heed those sorts of expressions, and take their cues for whatever came next.

"Students." Devon's eyes blinked back into focus as he shook his head dismissively at the room. "It's just students coming back to the campus."

The group of them stood there for a long, tense moment. Then, one by one, they started picking up the piles of paper littering the room. Silent apologies were both made and received as they did so. Help to retrieve a book. A silent nod from across the table. Angel briskly dusted the scorched pieces of her phone from her hands, and even handed Molly her coat as they got up to leave.

"Well, I'm glad we have a better idea of why she's doing it," Devon said quietly as they headed towards the door. "But it doesn't change the fact that we have no way of finding her."

"He's right," Gabriel said with a frown. "I mean...Samantha Neilson? We don't even know if that's her real name."

"It's her real name," Rae said confidently. "She *genuinely* admired us. She *genuinely* wanted us to be on her side. She told me her real name. But I don't see how that helps. I already tried using that tracking tatù on her, but I can't get a read. She has me blocked somehow."

"That's not surprising," Molly said comfortingly, nodding to a group of kids as they passed them on the lawn. "She could have whispered that to you at any time... From the second she perceived you as a possible threat."

"So where does that leave us?" Luke asked, slinging his arm around Molly's shoulder.

Rae thought about it for a moment before her eyes lit up with sudden illumination. "We might not have the power to find her, but I think I know someone who can at least point us in the right direction..."

One of the good things about being President of the Privy Council was that you got to summon anyone you wanted. And one of the good things about being President of *this* Privy Council, was that the people you tended to summon came equipped with superpowers.

The next afternoon, there was a knock on the door. Rae leapt to her feet to answer it, pulling it back to reveal a young man curiously staring inside.

"Curtis!" She gestured him in with a wide smile. "Come on in!"

"Thanks." He shook off his rain-drenched jacket and ventured into the foyer, gazing up with wide eyes at the decadent house. "You guys never do anything halfway, do you?"

Rae followed his gaze with a gracious chuckle as both Devon and Julian came down the stairs to greet him as well. As the men shook hands and made small talk Rae looked the newcomer up and down, trying to remember the last time she had seen him.

It had probably been the night of the Royal Ball. The one that went so terribly wrong. The one where a member of their own task force ended up kidnapping the future Queen of England.

Let bygones be bygones, right?

Curtis had been tasked with their surveillance and security. A task for which he was particularly well-suited, seeing as how the man had a way of seeing a bit of everything. Granted, it wasn't exactly in the way you might expect...

"So," Rae interrupted the little reunion as politely as she could, her eyes flickering automatically to the bag slung over his shoulder, "did you bring it?"

"Yeah." He reached down inside and extracted a silver disk. "This should fit any computer in the house. Although I don't really understand why you want it. I mean, you were there, Rae. Why do you need to look at an old surveillance tape?"

She was about to answer when he suddenly reeled back in horror.

"I mean—President Kerrigan."

Rae, Julian, and Devon stared at him for a split second before all three burst out laughing. It went on long and loud. Long enough to make the poor guy blush three times over.

"Seriously?" Devon gasped, clapping him on the shoulder. "*President* Kerrigan?"

"Please," Julian struggled to keep a straight face, "please tell me you weren't about to salute."

"Give me a break!" Curtis exclaimed, shoving them with a rueful grin. "She *is* the President of the Privy Council. How am I supposed to know what to call her?"

"Um...how about Rae?" she suggested lightly, trying her best not to smile. "You know, the same thing you've called me since you first met me. It also happens to be my name."

He rolled his eyes and backed away, grinning. "Well, if there was nothing else you wanted, Highness, I think I'll take my leave."

"Actually," Rae held out her hand with a hopeful grin, "there *was* something else I wanted."

She phrased it as a question. As an invitation. Just like she always did.

Having basically grown up with her, it took him only a second to understand. The next moment he was rolling up his sleeve, holding out his arm so she could wrap her fingers around it.

"I thought you already had mine," he said with a curious frown, staring down as if he could see the tatù leaving his body.

Rae shook her head, savoring the feeling as it coursed fresh through her veins.

"Long story. Needless to say, I lost a bunch of them all at once."

Courtesy of my long-lost brother.

Curtis nodded, as if this sort of thing happened all the time. Then he lifted his hand in a wave as he pulled open the door. "Well, best of luck to you guys. If what I saw at Guilder the other day is any indication, you guys are going to need it."

"That's it?" Devon asked in surprise. "You're just leaving? You just got here."

Curtis' eyes flickered quickly around the house, lingering on the closed doors and darkened hallways. "Yeah. No offense, guys, but I heard a rumor that Rae's dad was still lurking about on the premises. I think I'd rather just—"

"Absolutely not!" Rae tugged him forward, and shut the door. "My father is locked safely in the basement, I'll have you know. Just like in every other cozy little home. And the last thing I need is people thinking I'm using all my presidential currency to summon people for... I don't know...*tatù booty calls.*"

Devon stared at her for a moment, fighting back a smile. "Please don't call it that."

Curtis was unmoved, still warily looking around the house. "Are you sure? The last thing I want to do is get killed... or something."

"Don't be stupid, Curtis." Julian steered him towards the kitchen. "We ordered pizza."

After wolfing down three large pepperonis while reminiscing about old times, Curtis took Rae aside before heading out.

"Rae, my tatù's evolved slightly."

She raised an eyebrow, recalling the first time she had used it on Devon and watched him learn to ride his bike as a kid. He'd seen her in the memory. "Will it be the same for me? Or will it take time for me to use it as you do?"

"I'm not sure." Curtis scratched the back of his head. "Do you remember I used to have to use skin on skin in order to recall a memory?"

She nodded. "You were pretty adamant about that."

"Now I simply need to know someone. Or believe I know them well enough to step into the memory. I can't change outcomes—I don't think—but I've never changed the course of history. The ripples of time still find a way to smooth things out. You can use this ink without touching someone. At least, I can now. It might take time for you but, then again, it might not." He grinned apologetically. "You never cease to surprise me. I'm proud you're our president and you're going to make things right. I know it." He reached out his hand and Rae shook it, dazed at the faith Curtis had in her.

He left and Rae returned to the main room where everyone was. She grabbed the device Curtis had given her and set it up. The gang grew silent as they settled in to watch the tape.

There was no audio, apparently his hacking abilities hadn't progressed that far, but fortunately all Rae needed was a visual.

Sure enough, there was Samantha. Clutching a steaming cup of coffee as she made her way into Rae's interrogation room.

"She's so small," Devon murmured, clearly more upset by their present predicament than he was letting on. "I never realized how small she was before."

"Molly's small," Gabriel replied swiftly. "Look at all the damage she can do."

It was a rare compliment, and Molly met his eye across the table with an even rarer smile. At once, their little stand-off in the library was forgotten and they both settled in to watch the tape.

"Look. There we are talking," Rae narrated under her breath, watching the black and white figures go through something already firmly implanted in her memory, "and here is where she tells me to drink the coffee."

Right on cue, the second Samantha walked out the door, Rae picked up the mug and stared gulping it down like her life depended on it, thoroughly unaware that she had been supernaturally commanded to do so.

But it wasn't Rae's odd behavior that had everyone so transfixed. It was Samantha's.

"Did she really just..." Luke leaned forward incredulously and squinted at the screen. "Did she really just *wink* at the camera?"

"She knew we'd be watching," Angel said flatly, her eyes never leaving the monitor. "She knew we'd go back and dig up this footage. Girl's got style."

An echo of Jennifer Jones saying that exact same phrase echoed in Rae's mind and she shook her head quickly, freezing the video in place as she stared at the screen. She pressed hard into her memory of Samantha. Pretending the girl on the screen was in the room. While she'd never tried Curtis' power on a mere image before, already she could feel the ink working beneath her skin. Her heart began racing erratically but she pushed on, determine to use Curtis' ink in its more evolved form.

A second later, her eyes went blank and she slumped forward over the desk.

"Rae!" Gabriel cried.

She heard him but was too focused on what she intended to do to answer. She needed to find a memory of Samantha. Someone of the small girl's past to have a key to her future.

Devon caught her and gently set her down in the chair. "It's okay. Rae knows what she's doing. If she's somehow using Curtis' ability—which I have a feeling has changed—it takes her deep down into the subject's mind. Allows her to see a specific moment in their past. Sort of change it, in a sense. She's used it on me before. Once."

"Is that why she can't use Carter's ink?" Molly's voice dropped to a whisper. "Or is she still afraid to use it? Like him being gone make the ability taboo?" She didn't wait for anyone to answer, instead sweeping back her friend's hair and securing it in a quick braid. "Carter's only observed. It must be that."

Gabriel stared nervously at Rae, pacing back and forth in front of the desk.

Rae wanted to tell him it was going to be alright but was terrified the bond she was using with her own memories of Samantha, using Curtis' ink, would be severed. The original form of the ink, with the skin on skin contact, had been the only one she'd used before. This was new territory.

"Well, how long until she comes out of it?" Gabriel demanded. "Or what if she messes up something in the past, changes something she didn't mean to? It's the butterfly effect, right? What if she sets off a chain of events, and the next thing we know one of us isn't standing here?"

Julian settled on the opposite sofa with a soft smile. "You know, for how callous you are you certainly worry a lot." Gabriel opened his mouth for a scathing reply but Julian beat him to it, tapping the side of his temple. "If she's about to do anything wrong or permanent, I'll see. We'll knock her out or something before it happens."

"Knock her out?" Devon repeated slowly, turning around to stare at his friend.

Julian shrugged and flashed him a quick smile. "Or something."

Chapter 8

Down, down, and further down Rae travelled. She lost focus of the others in the room and centered herself only on finding Samantha's memories, or one of them. Falling through a blur of colors and detached memories. Flying so fast, Rae thought she might never reach the bottom.

Curtis' power worked differently than Carter's. Not just in theory, but in effect.

Carter's ability to delve into a person's mind felt like a pull. A deep pull that tugged at your very bones until you had no choice but to follow.

Curtis' felt like a shove. Like some unseen force was driving you with unspeakable power from behind. Pushing you farther and farther down, until the memory itself became your only salvation.

Rae sucked in a quick gasp of air and threw out her hands to brace for a landing, well aware that in the real world she probably hadn't moved at all. Her hair whipped out around her, and for a moment she felt a wave of sheer panic that she might never be able to stop.

But then, just as quickly as she'd slipped inside, she came to a crashing halt.

"*Ouch!*" she gasped, coming down hard upon a stiff carpet. The world around her blinked in and out of focus as a tiny smear of blood leaked down from her smashed nose.

Then she remembered that she could be seen, and quickly darted behind a door.

She was in a house of some sort. A nice house, from the looks of things. But quiet. Far too quiet. Considering the pictures of a family lining the wall, it was far too quiet indeed.

Then a single sound broke the silence. The sound of a door opening and then slamming shut. Soon followed by the uneven patter of little footsteps.

Rae cringed farther behind the door, wishing she had found a better hiding spot, when a tiny child raced inside the room. She was small. Unnaturally small. Rae had never noticed it before.

Samantha.

"Daddy! Daddy!" she squealed, her hands dripping a steady stream of mud onto the crisp white carpet. "Daddy, look what I've got!"

The unfortunate grasshopper in question had already slipped away unnoticed, but that's not what caught Rae's attention. *Daddy?* Confused, she followed the girl's gaze to a tall chair in the corner facing the window. At first, nothing happened. Then Rae spotted a single wisp of hair.

She sucked in a silent gasp, her heart pounding in her chest. She hadn't even realized he was sitting there. She'd never seen anyone so lifeless, so still. For a split second, she was terrified that he'd heard her speak when she first crashed inside, but on second thought she felt sure he hadn't.

She wasn't sure what exactly was wrong with this man, but he was in his own world. Lost and immune to everything going on around him. Including the little girl who'd just raced inside.

"Daddy?"

A look of extreme disappointment flashed through her dark eyes at his lack of reaction but, even so, she seemed to be expecting it somehow. Instead of retreating to the door she raced forward, spinning the chair around so that her father was facing the rest of the room.

For the second time, Rae clapped a hand over her mouth so she wouldn't be heard.

Lifeless.

She'd used the word before she'd even seen his face. Thinking only of how unnaturally still the man had become. But seeing him now, there was truly no better descriptor.

There was nothing remotely alive about him. No light in his pale green eyes. No sign that he'd even registered the chair had been turned around. If it wasn't for the faint movement of his chest, Rae would have sworn he had stopped breathing.

He was handsome. Or at least, he might have been handsome if his every feature didn't look like it had been carved from chilled stone. His skin had the unnatural pallor of someone who had been kept too long indoors, and judging by the deep grooves worn into the carpet he had been sitting in that chair for a long time.

But that wasn't the only confusing thing about him. It was the little pieces that didn't quite fit with the rest. The vague hints at a previous life—a life before the chair.

The snake tattoo that laced up around his wrist, barely visible beneath the cuff of his sleeve. The slightly paler skin circling his finger where a wedding ring once was. The pictures on the walls around him. Pictures of a man who thrived on adrenaline. A man in every country, in any number of situations, with every possible assortment of friends.

Skydiving. Backpacking. Drunken bonfires. A beautiful girl kissing his cheek.

Always smiling. Always moving. Always a second away from grabbing the camera.

Pictures that had long been blanketed in a layer of dust.

Rae didn't know how to reconcile it. Couldn't imagine what had possibly happened to make the man in the pictures the same man she was seeing today.

And yet, despite it all, there was something strangely familiar about him. Like she had seen his face somewhere before...

"Sammie?" he spoke suddenly, startling both girls. Blinking like a man coming out of a deep sleep. A man who would rather be back there. "What are you doing here? I thought you were at your aunt's."

Samantha paused, looking him up and down in an appraising sort of way. Then she fixed a cheerful smile on her face—a smile that was just as false as she was too young to have known it.

"That was last week." Her voice was like a tiny, chirping bird. A childlike precursor to the cartoonish lilt she had today. "This week, I was going to spend a couple days with you. Remember?"

The man's eyes clouded over, and he ran a hand up through his unkempt curls. "No...I don't."

Samantha flinched, but never lost hold of that smile. "That's okay, Daddy." She took him by the hand, having completely forgotten that her own was covered in mud. "Have you eaten anything today? I could make you something."

The child taking care of the parent. A five-year-old girl, with a thirty-year-old man.

He didn't answer, but seemed hesitant to move so far away from the window. The second he registered it he pulled himself gently free, not noticing the mud any more than his daughter. "I'm fine, Samantha. Why don't you go and play?"

Her eyes lit up with a surge of hope. The kind of hope that had dimmed through years of constant disappointment, but refused to completely die. The kind of hope that only hurt you. "Will you come with me?"

For a split second, his handsome face showed a flicker of life. A deep shining regret slowly made its way to the surface, followed by the most exquisite pain. "You go, honey," he said softly. "I'll...I'll watch from here." His finger flicked gently underneath her chin before he settled himself back down, turning the chair back to face the dusty window. Settling the castors back into their groove.

Samantha stared after him for a long moment before she turned suddenly on her heel and darted away, quickening her escape lest her father see that she'd started to cry.

Not that he'd notice. Not that he saw anything through that dirty glass.

Rae's heart broke as she stared through the slit in the door, watching as Samantha raced down the hall and headed back outside. At this point, she wasn't sure which one of them she was supposed to follow. But something told her to stay with the man.

There was something more to him than met the eye. Something lingering just beneath the surface, just waiting for her to remember.

She pulled in another quiet breath and prepared to wait it out, but no sooner had Samantha left the house than the chair spun back round. The man leapt to his feet with a speed and grace that Rae didn't think he was capable of, peering through the window until he saw the top of her little pigtails bobbing up and down in the yard.

A sad smile twisted up the corners of his lips, sticking there for a moment like his mouth didn't really know what to do. A soft sigh wilted his shoulders, and in a move so swift and sweet that Rae could hardly understand it he kissed his fingers before pressing them to the glass.

Then he was on the move.

Rae cringed further behind the safety of the door as he reached across the desk and picked up his cell phone. He stared at the buttons for a moment, as if trying to remember which ones to press, before typing a quick message onto the screen. It sent with a cheerful little *ding*.

The second it went out, he pulled a key from his pocket and reached to the bottom drawer in his desk. His face, already pale, grew whiter still as his fingers touched upon something cold.

...What are you doing?

Rae shifted uneasily, watching a series of micro-expressions dance across his face. What started out as uncertainty sharpened to fear, before giving way to a resolved sort of determination.

Seriously, man, what're you doing?

Her toes curled in her shoes as she was plagued with the sudden, unshakable feeling that something was about to go very wrong.

That's when he pulled out the gun.

No, no, no! This is not good! Samantha—come back!

But in the seconds that followed, Rae suddenly wanted Samantha to stay as far away from her father as possible. She felt sure that the message he'd sent was to the girl's aunt, asking the woman to come and collect her. And judging by the way he was staring down at the weapon, she also felt dreadfully sure that the man was never going to leave the room alive.

Do I stop him? Her mind raced desperately as they lived those final few seconds together. *Is that why I'm here? To stop him from committing suicide?*

Three times, she almost bolted from her hiding place to snatch the weapon away.

Three times, she stopped herself.

You cannot change time. Not something this big. Not when you don't know the consequences.

"I told you..."

Rae jumped in her skin as the man's voice rang out across the room. Strong this time. A far cry from the hollow murmur he'd used with his daughter.

At first, she was afraid he was talking to her. But his eyes were fixed upon the gun, staring so hard into the reflection it was as if he could see someone staring back.

"I told you I would never make it out of here alive."

He took a breath. Closed his eyes. And lifted it to his temple.

"I was right."

"*NO!*"

Rae's scream rang out at the exact same moment that the shot fired. One masked the other as both rang out through the house.

She was still screaming when her eyes snapped open and she found herself back in her living room in Kent. The last thing she saw were six concerned faces before her chair tipped backwards and she felt herself falling to the floor.

A pair of strong arms caught her.

"Rae!" Devon's hair spilled into his face as he stared down at her, his bright eyes wide with worry and alarm. "What happened?! Are you alright?!"

"Should've knocked her out," Gabriel murmured. "She changed something."

Luke shot him a look as Rae pulled in a gasp of air and sat bolt upright. The room around her wouldn't stop spinning, and her ears were still ringing with the crack of the gun.

"He killed...he killed..."

She couldn't finish the sentence. Couldn't even catch her breath enough to try. Her entire body was caught in a wave of shivers, and it wasn't until the room went dark that she realized Devon had pulled her up into his arms.

"It's okay," he soothed, smoothing her hair while she buried her face into his chest. "You're here now. You're safe. It's all over."

A dry sob ripped out of her and she pulled back, her eyes spilling over with tears. "I saw him do it," she wept, unable to stop herself. "I was standing right there."

"Who, baby?" Devon bent down a little so they were at eye level, scanning her face with a practiced skill that had been taught by the Council long ago. "Who killed himself?"

Rae shook her head, unable to pull herself together. "I should have stopped it. I should have—"

"No, you shouldn't have." Devon took her firmly by the shoulders and forced her to look up into his eyes. "Rae, no matter who he was you could not risk changing history that much, do you hear me? You could not have possibly saved his life."

Almost instinctively, Rae glanced at Julian. Desperate for a second opinion.

He caught her staring and shook his head, offering a sad but reassuring smile. "You don't want to go messing with the future like that. Trust me."

As she nodded her head shakily Molly slid in beside Devon, silently taking her hand. "Who died, Rae? What did you see?"

Rae pulled in a steadying breath, her eyes still adjusting to the dim lighting in the room.

"Samantha's father." Another shudder ran through her body as she remembered. "I went back to their house. Samantha couldn't have been more than five years old. She ran inside, trying to get him to play with her, but he was just...gone."

"He was already dead?" Devon asked. A strange look of relief washed over his face. "That's good. That means you didn't have to see it."

"No," Rae murmured, reaching back to touch the inexplicable braid tumbling between her shoulder blades, "he wasn't dead when I got there. He was just...gone. I don't know how else to say it. The man was dead inside. It's like something killed him already."

Or someone.

"But his face," she continued suddenly, "I knew his face. It was like I had seen him somewhere before. Except...I don't know how that would have been possible."

"If Samantha was five, we were only a few years older than that." Molly shook her head sadly, giving Rae's wrists a squeeze. "So, that's when he did it? When Samantha ran inside?"

Rae shook her head. "No. He sent her out first. I think...I think he loved her a great deal. He just...couldn't cope. It was like something had broken him. Broken him in a way that he could never be fixed. The second she was gone...he pulled out a gun and shot himself."

Julian and Devon looked away at the same instant, bowing their heads. Molly and Luke exchanged a quick look, while Angel and Gabriel were grim but unsurprised.

But that's not all he did...

"But wait. First, he...he talked to the gun."

Six pairs of eyes shot back at the same time, absorbing this sudden revelation as well as they could. Clearly, it left quite a lot to be desired.

"He talked to the gun?" Devon repeated, giving his fiancée every benefit of the doubt. To his credit, they had seen stranger things before. "What did he say?"

"He said..." Rae stared off into space as she remembered, hearing an echo of the dying man's final words. "He said, 'I told you I would never make it out of here alive...I was right.'"

It was in that precise moment that Rae realized where she had seen the man before. Why his handsome, hollow face had already been burned into her mind.

It was recent. Very recent. In fact, it had happened just the other day in a courtroom.

... within her father's memories.

"Rae, wait!"

The others tore after her, slipping into helping powers if they were able—anything to try to keep up with her frantic pace. But it was no use. The second the image struck home Rae sprang to her feet and stormed from the living room like the hounds of hell were behind her, making her way down to the basement.

"Rae, please slow down." Devon was the only one able to catch up to her, and even he seemed a bit out of sorts as to what to do, not that he had done so. "Just think about this for a minute. Whatever you do, it shouldn't be done in anger."

"Why not?" she snapped, hardly breaking her stride. "Why shouldn't things be done to my father *out of anger*? I tend to think it would be quite fitting considering the things he's done himself!"

"Rae, come on." He grabbed her by the arm and spun her back around, giving the others a chance to catch up. They were standing in the kitchen, right by the stove. Rae on one side. And all the rest skidding to a stop on the other.

"Just tell us what's going on," Devon reasoned, raising his hands calmingly in the air. He was neither stopping nor helping her plan, he simply wanted to understand it. "One second you're just sitting there, talking about this man's suicide. The next, you're storming down to the basement on a revenge mission to murder your own father."

The words echoed back and forth across the high ceilings, coming back darker and graver every time. They reflected in the faces of everyone gathered around, but none so much as on the young man who had just walked through the door.

The same man now frozen on the spot. "WHAT?"

Everyone whipped around at the same time. Staring open-mouthed at Kraigan as he paused incredulously in the frame. Rae's eyes widened upon seeing him, and for a split second she felt a burning stab of shame.

Kraigan. What was I thinking?

No one had thought to look for him after the battle at Guilder. In the chaos and personal turmoil that had followed, he hadn't crossed a single person's mind. Kraigan was in the unique position of having literally no one else in his corner. Since the fight at the factory Rae had grown strangely protective of him, and the two had developed an uneasy truce—but it wasn't the same thing. Kraigan quite simply wasn't on anyone's radar. He had worked so hard to evade it for so long that carving out a niche for himself had proven a near impossible feat.

Ironically, it was one of the few things he shared with his father.

"Kraigan... hey." Devon stepped forward quickly, looking similarly mortified at such a fundamental lapse. "We didn't...uh...why don't you come in?"

But Kraigan remained where he stood. Frozen in shock. Staring, dumbstruck, at his sister. "Dad's still here?" he repeated, glancing towards the basement. "Why would he...I thought that after the trial...I thought he'd be gone."

He and Rae locked eyes.

One of them, searching desperately for answers.

The other, having no idea in the world what he was trying to say.

"Kraigan," Rae began carefully, temporarily losing sight of Simon amidst the sudden appearance of his son, "where have you been?"

For the first time, Kraigan took a step back. His cheeks flushed with something as close to guilt as a man like him was capable, before he strode suddenly inside and shut the door behind him. "I left the courthouse," he said simply. "The second the first witness took the stand. The second it became clear that, no matter what happened that morning, they were going to execute our father that afternoon. A fact guaranteed by your promise, dear sister, to always tell the truth."

Neither sibling was willing to blink first. Neither willing to back down.

But the longer Kraigan stood there, the quicker his anger gave way again to that initial astonishment that had stopped him on the way in. "Dad's here," he said again. This time, it wasn't a question. It was his own personal miracle, one he was only beginning to comprehend. "You didn't...I mean, *they* didn't kill him?"

Rae's throat tightened, and she turned her head away. She couldn't answer. She couldn't even find it in herself to look at him.

He simply didn't know.

He didn't know anything that had happened since they'd set foot in the courtroom that fateful morning. He didn't know about the fight afterwards. Or how their father had been given a temporary reprieve. He didn't know that there was a crazy person after them—again—or that she had already infiltrated the gang enough to have temporarily torn them apart.

He didn't even know that Rae had advocated for life.

Life for Simon. Unlike the lives he so carelessly took away.

And on that note...

"Yeah," Rae said shortly. "Dad's here. He's in the basement. And I would talk to him while you can, Kraigan. Because I'm about to remedy that situation shortly."

While Kraigan froze uncertainly, Devon stepped into her line of sight.

"But why?" he said again. "You still haven't told us—"

"That man I saw didn't kill himself. He was murdered a long time ago. What I was looking at was just the shell that got left behind." She straightened up to her full height. Turning slowly to face the basement. "And the man who killed him...was Simon Kerrigan. My father. Kraigan's father. He's not innocent. Of anything."

Chapter 9

Since Rae woke up on her sixteenth birthday and discovered she had superpowers, she stopped using doorknobs when she was angry. She preferred to kick the whole thing down instead.

"Simon!!"

Dad was gone. The word 'Dad' would never pass through her lips again.

Simon leapt to his feet as the splintered planks rained down around him, gazing up in shock as he watched his daughter storm down the stairs. Her half-brother was right behind her. As were the rest of her bewildered friends. None of them seemed to know what was going on any more than he did.

Rae knew. She saw the bewilderment in Simon's face, Kraigan's, Devon's, and everyone else's. No one got it—except maybe Gabriel and Angel.

"Rae? What is it?" Simon took a tentative step forward, then stopped, bracing most likely against the look of pure fury flashing in her eyes. "What happened?"

She didn't answer him. She turned to Julian instead.

"If I give you a paper, can you draw me a face?" She conjured the items even as she asked the question, shoving them into his chest. "The same man I just saw?"

He caught them automatically, but shook his head. "You saw him in the past, in *his* past. I can't—"

"What if I decide to think about him again?" she insisted. Her voice trembled with so much pent-up emotion, it seemed constantly on the edge of bursting forth. "If I decide to sit down and relive everything I just saw. Could you do it then?"

Julian cast a quick glance at Devon, but found no help. "No...I couldn't." His eyes dropped apologetically to the tools she'd conjured, still clutched uselessly against his chest. "Rae, I'm sorry. I would just see you sitting there, thinking about it. I couldn't see what was actually going on inside your mind—"

"*Jules.*" Those emotions flared up, and she fought to keep them under control. "I need you to try for me, okay? I need you to sit down and just try. Please." In a fit of impatience, she actually pushed him down at a desk shoved into a corner, taking back the pen just long enough to thrust it once more into his hand. The paper was soon to follow. "Please," she said again, preemptively cutting him off before he could speak. "*Please*, Jules."

Julian's eyes flickered swiftly between her and Simon before lowering helplessly to the paper. The pen twisted instinctually in his hand. As for the rest, he didn't know where to begin. "Rae," he murmured, "there's nothing for me to center on—"

"Center on me," she said quickly, perching on the edge of the desk. She peered down at him in the dim lighting, completely ignoring her father hovering obliviously in the back. "Center on me sitting upstairs—travelling back there in my mind. Imagine me doing it again."

With a look of extreme patience Julian closed his dark eyes, lifting his chin slightly as he waited for the future to reveal itself to him. But this wasn't the future they were talking about. It was the past. And that patience was quick to fade.

Rae sighed, already knowing what was happening. Or, what wasn't happening.

The pen twitched in Julian's hand, and his brow creased into a frustrated frown. Finally, after a full minute of trying, he gave up and opened his eyes—eyes just as dark and dilated as before. "I'm sorry," he said softly. "I can't."

Rae tossed her hair impatiently, slamming her hand against the paper. "Yes, you can!"

"Rae," Devon interjected quietly, coming to his friend's aid, "you know that's not how his power works—"

"We've progressed before," she said shortly. "Jules especially. He can do it again."

"On command?" Molly inserted with a bit of a reprimand. "He can't see inside your head."

But Rae didn't listen to any of them. There was too much riding on this to be dissuaded now. Too much at stake to simply give up and walk away. Instead, she leaned forward and rested her hand atop Julian's, staring intently into his lovely eyes. "Yes...you can."

There was something different in her voice this time as she said it. A strange intensity, as calming as it was persuasive. Perhaps it was for this reason that Julian decided to try again.

This time was slightly different than before.

He took a deep breath, bracing himself slightly against the table. Then, without seeming to think about it, he reached out and took her hand.

That's it...you've got it...

There wasn't a sound in the room. Even Simon had frozen perfectly still as the circle of friends gazed down as one to stare at the psychic.

And that's when it happened.

"Jules..."

Rae didn't know which one of them said it. Whose gasp it was that rang out in the quiet corners of the little room. But whoever it was, she didn't blame them in the slightest. Whatever was happening to their clairvoyant friend, it was truly a sight to behold.

As if he was moving in slow motion, Julian lifted his chin as every speck of color drained out of his eyes. Instead of taking on their usual glassy hue they were almost translucent, giving off a faint glow that cast shadows off his high cheekbones and long hair. Before long, his entire body was awash with it. Rigid, yet relaxed. Physically anchored in place as his mind reached out through space and time. Breaking boundaries. Flying through entire worlds the rest of them would never see.

"What's happening to him?" Angel whispered, taking a step forward. "Is he alright?"

Gabriel held her back, but Devon stepped forward as well. He looked half in awe, half so worried that he was just seconds away from trying to intervene.

Rae beat him to it. "Jules?" She leaned closer, studying him carefully for any signs of distress. "Are you okay?"

He didn't answer her. Gave no indication that he'd even heard.

Then suddenly, without any warning, his hand clamped down onto hers, gripping it so hard it was all she could do to stop herself from crying out.

"Jules," she gasped, trying to twist herself free.

She'd never known he was so strong. That his ink could make him so strong. Truth be told, she was willing to bet he didn't know it either.

She tried again to pull herself free, but it was like trying to fight a statue. A statue that resembled a glowing version of her best friend. A statue that happened to be breaking her hand.

"Rae?" Devon came up behind her, his voice thick with tension. "What's happening?"

She just shook her head, wincing slightly as she stared into Julian's blank face. "I don't know, but I can't get out. It's like he's—"

It was only then that she realized what he was trying to do. Understood the connection that his unconscious mind was striving to build.

Of course!

What did Carter's ink, Curtis' ink, even Maria's telepathic ink all have in common? They all started developing via physical contact. If Julian was trying to make some kind of psychic connection now, it would make sense that it would develop in the same way.

That being said, at this rate it was likely to break her...

A hundred different tatùs flashed through her mind, each one offering themselves up for assistance. But in the end, the decision wasn't up to her. Like it usually did in times of stress, her body chose of its own accord—summoning the ink to the surface with a familiar little hum.

Let's see if this is up to the challenge...

With a burst of strength Rae stopped trying to fight the grip, and embraced it instead. Her fingers laced through Julian's, and without thinking she reached out with her other hand.

The power she'd chosen was nothing but strength. Unbridled, impossible strength. The kind of strength that would have crushed Julian's bones in a second had he not been in a trance. But now, somehow, his body was able to withstand it. And not just withstand it, but match it with his own.

"I can't believe this is happening," Molly murmured.

But Rae was too far removed to answer her. From the second she and Julian locked hands, it was as if her mind was no longer her own. Her eyes snapped shut, and without making the decision to go there herself she was suddenly transported back. Back down the shadowy recesses of her mind. Back into those memories she had tried so hard to forget.

It was one of the strangest sensations she had ever felt. Not like the push of Curtis' ability, not like the pull of Carter's. If she had to guess, she would say that Julian wasn't influencing any of this. He had simply established some sort of psychic connection, and was allowing her to go there herself—looking on as a silent observer.

She tried to help as best she could. Thinking back to the pristine study, tainted only with a child's trail of mud. Thinking back to the look on Samantha's face, to the unspeakable hurt and disappointment written there. And then, finally, the chair turned around and she saw the man.

The gun cracked. A spray of blood splashed across his lifeless face.

Julian flinched at the sound. Then grew very still.

For a full minute, they shared a suspended connection. For a full minute they sat silently together, staring unblinkingly into each other's eyes.

Then, just as quickly as it started, it was over.

Julian released her, and with a speed so fast that even she could hardly follow his hand started flying across the blank page.

Rae blinked quickly and shook her head to clear it. Her mind was still spinning from what she'd just seen, and it was a few seconds before she could focus again on the room.

"Honey?" Devon knelt in front of her, smoothing her fingers automatically to check for breaks and damage. "Are you okay? What—what the hell is going on?"

"He saw him," she breathed, beaming with pride as she stared at Julian's face. His eyes were still completely blank, yet glowing. The image on the page was slowly taking shape. "He saw the man's face. He can draw him. I would never have been able to..." Even as she said it, there was a rustling of paper.

As Julian's fingers whipped back and forth across the desk, blurring with speed, the likeness of a man appeared beneath them.

Like all of Julian's work, it was drawn to perfection. More of a photograph than a sketch.

Despite having never seen him in person, and the fact that the man died over ten years ago, Julian was somehow able to capture every detail. The pale skin beneath the missing ring. The handsome, yet hollow features. The lifeless eyes. He'd even gotten the guy's tattoo.

Just a few seconds later, it was finished. The gang looked on in wonder as he slowly pushed it across the table, dropping the pen and closing his eyes. He rubbed them for a moment, as if the entire ordeal was very tiring, then slowly, ever so slowly, he returned to the present.

"Welcome back," Rae said with a smile. She held up the page. "You did it."

He blinked in disorientation, trying to get his bearings. "...I did?"

She nodded as Devon swooped in to attend to him before slowly getting to her feet and approaching her father. The smile was quick to fade. The rage was quick to return.

As she held it up in front of him, her hand trembled with it. "You know him." It wasn't a question. There was no doubt in her mind. "I saw him in your memory, back at the courthouse. I *know* you know him."

She expected him to deny it. For him to think up some quick, yet charming excuse to get her to dismiss it like he always did.

But he didn't.

The second he saw the page his face went white with shock. He reached out with a hand trembling just as much as hers, and traced the edges of it. "Elias."

Rae leaned forward, making sure she didn't miss a single word.

"What? Elias?" Her eyes flashed as the crack of the gun echoed again in her mind. "Who's Elias? How do you know him?"

But Simon was too surprised for an interrogation. He tuned out her questions completely, staring in unmitigated shock at the drawing. "How do *you* know him?" he countered, unable to move his gaze. "What did you see?"

For a moment, Rae almost paused. She'd glimpsed only enough of this Elias in her father's memory to be certain the two shared an acquaintance. And she knew enough of her father's acquaintances to know that most of them ended up dead.

"What did I see?" she repeated through clenched teeth. In her periphery Kraigan moved a step closer, prepared to jump between them. "I saw a man completely and utterly destroyed. A man's whose life stopped mid-swing. Whose insatiable passion for everything the world had to offer was suddenly taken away from him."

Simon said nothing. But for the first time, he was looking in her eyes.

"That man is Samantha's father. And I watched him put a gun to his head and kill himself while..." her voice cracked as she thought about herself and the fire that had once killed her parents, "while his five-year-old daughter played outside."

There was a heavy silence, punctuated by a harsh scrape of a chair.

Rae dragged it to the center of the room, then pointed with an accusatory finger. "Sit. Talk. Don't even think about leaving something out." She lifted the same finger to point it at his chest. "I used Carter's power once. If I have to I'll do it again."

There was that presidential tone again. The one that had gotten her elected. The one that popped up at random moments, taking charge when things spiraled too far out of control.

Simon watched her for a second, then sank down onto the chair. He took a moment to settle himself, then lifted his chin to look her straight in the eye. "What do you want to know?"

Rae paced back and forth, keeping him locked in her gaze all the while. "How did you know Elias? What was he to you?"

"Elias is—*was*—one of the most powerful telepaths I'd ever met." For a second, a look of true sorrow flashed in Simon's eyes. Rae couldn't tell whether it was from the loss of life, or from the loss of ink that followed. "We met at a bar. I guess you could say I searched him out."

"Searched him out for what?" Rae fired back. They were up against the clock. She didn't have time for half-truths or missing details.

"You know for what." Simon's gaze leveled with hers, bringing an unintentional pause to her pacing.

Yes. She certainly did know what. She had seen the storage warehouse for herself. She had seen the cells full of people. Lab rats for experimentation. Row after row of hollow, empty faces. So many faces that the lot of them became a blur.

But still. The second she saw Elias...she should have known.

"What did you do to him?" she muttered, still trying to reconcile the beaming face of the man in the pictures with the lifeless corpse she found on the floor.

"The same thing I did to all of them," Simon said softly. "Studied his ability in various situations, under various levels of stress. Gave him drugs to enhance it." He paused slightly, eyes tightening as he remembered. "The study expanded when he had a child."

Rae froze in her tracks, feeling as though the entire world had melted away and it was just the two of them. She and her father. And all these terrible secrets.

"When he had a child?" she repeated darkly.

She had seen the circumstances under which people in her father's clutches were made to have children. It was something she wished she could forget.

Simon bowed his head. "I didn't know the child had survived. I don't know any of them did. To be honest," he hesitated, considering whether he should say the next part, "I kind of assumed they had starved."

Rae looked up in horror. The interrogation temporarily stopped.

And she wasn't the only one unable to comprehend such atrocities...

There was a quiet gasp from the back of the room. Molly had backed all the way into Luke's chest—one hand on her belly, looking like she was about to be sick. She and Rae locked eyes for a moment before Rae gave her the briefest of nods. The next second, she was up the stairs and out of the basement entirely. Luke was fast on her heels.

No one else moved. As much as they might have wanted to bolt from the house and never return, they were rooted to the spot. All staring with the same expression. All holding their breath.

"They *didn't* survive," Rae said coldly, bringing them back on topic. "Even if you didn't kill them outright—you still killed them. It just took a while for the bullet to hit." She took a step closer. Towering down over her father as little wisps of smoke started trailing dangerously from her hands. "Elias told you himself, didn't he?" Her hands balled into fists as the man's tragic, final words echoed in her mind. "He said he'd never make it out of that place alive." The smoke brightened with flames. "Well, guess what, Simon...he didn't."

No one said anything for a long time. After a revelation like that, what could you say?

Angel and Gabriel were standing like twin sentries, each of them frozen in the same defensive pose on either side of the doorway. Julian was still slumped back against the desk, staring at Simon like he was a nightmare come to life. Devon had one hand gripped supportively on his shoulder, but he, too, seemed at a total loss for words.

This was the same man who had helped him back at Guilder? This was the same man who'd fathered the love of his life?

Even Kraigan had enough sense to keep quiet. He was still standing close enough to Rae to intervene if things got violent, but there was an uncharacteristically troubled expression shadowing his face. As if there were some things in this world that even he was unable to reconcile.

Finally, when it could go on no longer, Simon cleared his throat. "Rae, I've never tried to hide the darkness in my past. You've always known—"

"Yes, but now your past has come back to kill us." Rae's voice cracked out like a whip, slicing the air between them. "Once again, my future is being crushed under the sheer weight of your sins." *The sins of the father are the sins of the son, or in this case the daughter.* Uncle Argyle had it right all along.

Simon sucked in a quick breath, bowing his head to his chest before staring back up into the eyes of his daughter. Into the eyes of his son. "I'm sorry." It looked like he was dying to get up out of the chair. Dying to embrace them. But a lifetime's worth of tragedy stood in his way. "I can never...never tell you how very sorry I am. If there was anything I could do—"

"It isn't us you have to apologize to," Rae said flatly. "It's a whole lot of dead people."

Kraigan shot her a quick look, but stayed silent.

"You're right," Simon conceded, shaking his head. "And I've wished every single day for a long time that was possible. I wish I could go back in time and do things differently. Live without the lies, without the secrets. Without this blood on my hands. I wish I could undo every bit of damage I've caused. I wish I could have been there to watch you grow up. Given you the lives you deserve." His face tightened once more as he stared his children up and down. "I wish I could have been a father to you."

Kraigan's hands were trembling as he broke eye contact and bowed his head.

Rae, however, stared right back at Simon. Stared with eyes just as hollow and lifeless as Elias. "Well...you can't."

She headed up the stairs without another word.

Without stopping.

Without looking back.

"You can't."

Chapter 10

There are psychological ramifications to days like this. Days like this leave scars that can't be ignored.

Even when they were back at Guilder, after having witnessed the rapidly unraveling mind of Madame Elpis, Rae had never fully appreciated the wisdom in her mother's words until this very moment.

In the last few days she'd been stabbed by the man she loved, seen every horror and atrocity her father had ever committed, watched as the fabric of her world was ripped apart in civil war, and then saw a young man, who should be brimming with hope and promise, shoot himself in the head.

It was too much.

It was all just too much.

And *that* was how Rae Kerrigan accidentally froze the world for a second time.

She certainly didn't mean to do it. She hadn't even realized she'd slipped into a different set of ink until she realized that all the people she'd been talking with had frozen behind her in the hall.

"...Which is why we need to get a replacement anklet as soon as possible. I have no idea why we let our precautions get so lax, but this isn't up for—Are you guys even listening?!" She whipped around in frustration, then stopped cold, her eyes widening in wonder as she gazed back at a hall of statues. "Guys?"

No one made a sound.

Rae took a cautious step forward, waving a hand in front of Gabriel's face. A second later, she reached out and tugged a lock of Angel's long hair. "...Guys?"

Nope. Nothing. Angel would have smacked her for the hair-tug.

"Oh crap," she muttered, running a hand up over her face. "Not again."

Her first thought was to try to reverse it somehow. She certainly couldn't leave them all just standing here mid-step. It seemed improper, though. And dangerous. Given everything that was happening, it could be very dangerous indeed.

It wasn't often this group of people were rendered helpless, but that was the overwhelming thought which struck Rae as she walked between them. They all looked so vulnerable. So exposed. At the complete mercy of the world around them. Unable to take care of themselves. Too dangerous.

Her next thought turned comical and she covered her mouth to hide the giggle. *What if I snap a pic?* It would be hilarious—sort of. She could prove to them that Julian wasn't the only one developing his powers. That she had a new set of ink up her sleeve as well. If it hadn't been for the fact that chaos seemed to haunt their every morning, she'd have told them already. *Plus, I have no idea how where it's come from. Who else has this ability? And freakin' knows how to use it!*

She reached for her phone in her back pocket and then shook her head. *Stupid! Stupid! Stupid! People freeze automatically in pictures!* So the rest of the super-gang would hardly see it as proof. *Maybe a video?*

Stop it, Kerrigan!! she scolded herself.

Her final assessment—the one she settled with—was to simply be overwhelmingly relieved that she had a moment just to herself. A minute where she wouldn't have to put on a show of strength or bravery. A minute where she wouldn't have to fret about being presidential, or spend it planning a defense against whatever was coming next.

For a suspended moment, she could just be Rae Kerrigan.

A girl who had recently graduated high school. Who had gone gallivanting around the world hunting for super-villains after that. Who had recently been proposed to, and in the wake of an overwhelming loss had yet to share the news with her own mother. A girl who was hailed as a freak amongst freaks. A supernatural outlier no matter what room she walked into. A girl with the ability to stop the progression of time if she wanted, just to give herself a minute like this.

... A minute to freak the heck out.

"HOW IS THIS MY LIFE?!"

She sank to her knees right there on the spot, in the middle of them, completely oblivious to the frozen people standing around her. They couldn't see her now. They couldn't worry or judge.

She knelt there for just a moment, fuming. And then, in a burst of anger, she jumped to her feet again and started kicking out the remaining planks of splintered wood from the frame of the basement door. Taking great care to hurl each one back down to her father, who sat frozen in the interrogation chair.

"HOW ARE YOU MY DAD?!"

When she ran out of planks she ran out of the hall, skidding to a stop under the vaulted ceiling by the front door. A place that would have the best natural amplification.

"HOW THE HELL IS THIS HAPPENING?!"

Again. How was it happening *again*?

Not the time-freezing. The immortal danger they always faced.

They had just been through this, hadn't they? They had just waged an epic war against an all-powerful lunatic set out to destroy their world. They had just beaten themselves down, torn themselves apart, and given up everything they had for the greater good. They had just lost people, lost themselves, put their lives on hold...all for what?

For it to happen all over again?!

With a half-strangled shriek, Rae ran to the stairs and started kicking the marble steps as hard as she could. Hair flying and chest panting as she gave in to the rage.

"The whole point of this freakin' Guilder place was so that we could get BETTER!" she shouted as she attacked the base of the stairs. "So we could learn to sleep without the freakin' LIGHTS ON!" She glared in the direction of the basement where Simon Kerrigan sat. "You told me to be scared of the monsters under my bed and in my closest! You're a bastard! You should have told me happily ever after fairytales and lied. Given me some false sense of security!" She stood a moment, huffing and catching her breath before she returned to kicking.

It was a good thing she wasn't still using a strength tatù. She might have collapsed the entire house in on itself. As it stood, the most she could break was her boot.

"And wouldn't that be perfect?" she challenged, abandoning the stairs altogether as she flew back across the checkered tile. "The perfect metaphor: a broken house. A broken house for broken people. People who never have a chance to get better."

Using every bit of strength she had, she threw open the front door and rushed out into the night, staring up at the starry sky with angry tears blurring her eyes.

"ARE YOU KIDDING ME?!"

She screamed aloud, waving her fists at the sky.

Screaming at nothing in particular. Screaming at everything all at once.

"WHAT MORE DO YOU WANT FROM ME?!"

As if to answer, an icy breeze stirred up her hair as every last bit of strength, energy, and fight left her body all at once. She sank to her knees once more, shivering slightly in the cold.

"What more can you take?" she whispered.

It was impossible to know how long she sat out there. Time was literally standing still, and even if it wasn't there would have been nothing to mark its passing. No noise by which to track the gradual shift of the hours.

The birds were frozen silent in the trees. The leaves turned statuesque, no longer rustling in the breeze. The only thing that was still moving was Rae herself, and she had long ago curled up into a little ball, pulling her knees to her chest as she let the darkness slowly devour her.

I wish I could have been a father to you.

It wasn't the kind of thing a girl who'd grown up without one could take lightly. The kind of thing Rae could let roll off her back or compartmentalize for another day.

It was tearing her apart.

Literally.

Her hand clutched at the recently ravaged skin that Alicia had healed the day before, gasping as though she could still feel it. As though there was still a giant hole in her chest. One that was letting all the cold air pour right inside.

Nothing helped. Nothing quieted her wracking sobs. Nothing even came close.

She wept until she could weep no more, and then quietly picked herself up and started walking back to the house. The door was still wide open, and as she closed it she bumped up the thermostat by several degrees. The entire house was freezing now, courtesy of her meltdown.

She went to take her place back amongst the others, but on the way she paused to look at her reflection in the hallway mirror.

Pale skin. Tear-stained cheeks. And the bloody weight of the world on her shoulders.

She pulled in a quick breath and straightened herself up as best she could. It wouldn't do for the others to see her this way. After all, this disaster was theirs to shoulder as well.

When she was finished, she took her place at the front of the frozen processional heading up the stairs to the living room. After glancing back to time out her footsteps with the others, she pulled in a deep breath, closed her eyes, and visually relaxed her magical grip on the hands of time.

A soft chorus of sound hit her first. Things so quiet, you never noticed them until they were taken away completely. The hum of the refrigerator, the quiet medley of a group of people breathing, the ticking of clocks.

Then Gabriel ran into her from behind.

"Are you okay?" His hands shot out to catch her. Apparently, her attempts to fall back in step with the rest of them weren't as brilliant as she thought. "Sorry, didn't realize I was going that fast."

"Yeah, it's okay." She blushed as she hurried forward. "I'm fine."

Out of the corner of her eye, she could have sworn Devon flashed her a strange look but, at the moment, they had bigger problems.

Simon was still one anklet short, Julian looked like someone had zapped seventy years off his life, and they now knew that Samantha had the perfect reason to hate them.

... and none of them had noticed they'd begun to shiver in the frigid house.

"Crap—sorry!"

Apparently, Rae wasn't the only one having balance problems. The second they made it up the stairs and safely out of the basement, Julian's waning strength finally gave out.

He threw out a hand to balance against the wall as his legs buckled beneath him. And missed, sending him crashing forward. Of course, Devon was right there to steady him. Except, for possibly the first time *ever*, that didn't exactly go as planned.

As Devon's arm shot out to grab him, Julian flinched away.

It was an automatic reflex. An unavoidable result of having had that same arm try to choke the life out of him just a day earlier. But Rae didn't miss it—it cut to Devon's very soul. Breaking his heart and searing into his memory forever.

An unnatural silence fell over the hall as best friends looked in opposite directions. Both boys pretending the moment had never happened. Both devastated that it had.

"Sorry," Julian mumbled again, pushing weakly to his feet, "I didn't mean—"

Devon's face tightened and he shook his head. "Don't. You have...you have every right."

They stood there for another moment, unable to meet each other's eyes.

Then Julian staggered a gracious step closer and reached out his arm. "Will you help me?"

Devon looked up with a truly unreadable expression. Their eyes met for a split second, then he hastily nodded. Taking great care to slow down his movements, he wound Julian's arm over his shoulder and, together, the two of them made their way down the hall.

The others stayed behind, staring after them.

For whatever reason, it struck Rae as a bad omen. An ominous harbinger of even more ominous things to come. One that rang true with every echoed step.

It struck all of them that way.

"Jules is dreaming about the bridge again," Angel murmured, staring after him with a deep sadness for one so young. "He had finally stopped... then came Guilder."

Rae shuddered and wrapped her arms around her chest. She could still hear the impacts like they were happening all over again. Fist on fist. Friend on friend.

Gabriel stared after them for a moment before slipping his arm around Angel's shoulder. "He'll be fine. He'll get over it." Without thinking about it, he stroked back her long hair, resting his cheek against the top of her head. "We all get over it."

She bit her lip, unable to tear her eyes away. "They're different than us," she murmured, seemingly oblivious to the fact that both Rae and Kraigan were still standing there. "Better, somehow."

Gabriel looked down sharply, tilting up her head. "Don't ever say that."

"It's true," she breathed. "You know it is. They don't get over things like this. They shouldn't." There was a slight pause. "We shouldn't either."

Gabriel didn't say anything. Perhaps there was nothing more to say. Instead, he simply tightened his grip on her shoulder and led her off down the hall, leaving brother and sister standing alone.

Rae wanted to follow, but her feet wouldn't move. While everyone else was free now to do whatever they pleased, it was she who was frozen. Staring after the rest of them as they set up in the living room, ready to tackle the night's new problem. She was slightly less ready.

"What happened at Guilder?"

She looked up suddenly to see Kraigan staring down at her. She hadn't realized how close he was, just a step or two away. After steering clear of each other so long, it still struck her as strange.

"We were attacked," she said quietly, feeling guilty again for not realizing that he wasn't there when it happened. "By a sixteen-year-old with the power of persuasion. She turned us against each other. Made us do..." An involuntary shudder rippled down her skin. "Made us do terrible things."

Kraigan's eyes lit with surprise, silently asking a million questions. But in the end, he settled only on one. The most important. The one he was most frightened to ask. "Simon's sentencing..."

It was Simon now, Rae noticed. Not 'Dad' for him either.

She turned without thinking and stared back at the basement door. The frame was now completely empty; all the loose planks had been cast down the stairs. Simon must still be sitting there, wondering what exactly had happened. Or maybe knowing what had. Rae had no idea what her father was and wasn't capable of anymore. Shoot, she couldn't even remember what tatù he was carrying now.

"What happened with his sentencing?" Kraigan asked again.

"I asked the court to let him live." Her eyes glazed over as she forced her mind forward, unwilling to imagine him for a second more. "They agreed. Life in prison."

Considering he was a man who wore his every violent emotion on his sleeve, Rae was actually having a hard time deciding how Kraigan felt about the news. The relief was palpable, that much was clear. But it was shadowed with so many other things, twisted with so many conflicting emotions, that it was hard to tell for sure.

After a moment of standing there, he finally bowed his head. "Thank you," he said simply. "For doing that."

Rae couldn't respond. Standing there now, she had no earthly idea whether she'd made the right decision.

Judging by Samantha's reaction, she'd have to say no.

Exhausted and devastated, she nodded curtly and moved to make her way down the hall to the living room

She hadn't gotten more than three steps, when Kraigan caught her by the sleeve. "Rae..."

She turned around in surprise, staring up at him. There was an uncertainty in his voice she'd never heard before, and an uncharacteristic blush was coloring the tops of his cheeks.

"I know...I know he's a terrible man. I know it's hard to have him in the house."

Her surprise doubled, but she kept it to herself. He was trying to go somewhere with this, trying very hard to work it all out. A little sisterly patience was in order.

"I don't..." He breathed hard through his nose, fighting back waves of doubt and an overwhelming feeling of frustration. "I don't..."

"I know." Rae put her hand on his arm, squeezing it gently as he forced himself to look her in the eye. They stared for a moment before she let out a soft sigh. "I know."

Then, in possibly the strangest turn of events to happen that fateful night, he slipped his hand into hers. For a second they both looked down, staring at their interlaced fingers. It was the first time brother and sister had ever shown such affection, and it would probably be the last. But there was something quite natural about it. Right then in the moment.

A faint smile lit Rae's face as she gave his fingers another squeeze. Maybe there was hope after all.

Then brother and sister made their way down the hall to the living room.

Hand in hand. Together.

The atmosphere in the living room had grown rather subdued by the time they made their way inside. Although Molly and Luke had joined them again, no one was in much of a mood to plan or strategize. Apparently, they were still reeling from the things they'd seen and heard in the basement. Rae could almost see the wheels turning inside everyone's mind. What had she done? What had she forced them to do? Was she turning into her father?

Everyone looked shocked. Not the least of which her best friend.

"What happened to you down there, Jules?" Molly asked quietly, swiveling around in her chair to look at Julian. The two of them usually sat together at these sorts of meetings. It was a subconscious habit, one that had been established long ago. "I've seen you have powerful visions before. I've seen them make you bleed. But I've never seen anything like that."

The others nodded, all remembering that strange translucent glow.

He pulled in a deep breath, trying to gather his thoughts despite looking so exhausted. He looked on the verge of losing consciousness. "I don't really know." He spoke quietly, considerately, his lips working it out as he went. "Rae needed it done, needed to show Simon the picture. So, I guess it kind of just... happened."

Rae shook her head, profoundly touched by such an innate show of loyalty. "You blow me away," she said sincerely. "Honestly, Jules. There's no one better."

Angel smiled proudly and took his hand while Devon flashed him a faint grin from across the room.

Julian, predictably, looked incredibly uncomfortable with all the attention. "Yeah, but, given what Simon said when he saw it," he circled them back on point, "I think we're going to have an even worse time with this girl than we thought."

The group shuddered as one, and murmured their agreement.

How were they supposed to dissuade a girl whose father Simon had kidnapped and tortured? A girl whose very existence was forced into the world at gunpoint? Who never even stood a chance?

"I don't know." Rae shook her head, suddenly feeling very tired. "A part of me thinks that we should just stick a bow on him and leave him out by the gate. Toss in a tag with Samantha's name on it."

"Well, that wouldn't be very sporting of you, would it?"

The entire room jumped as a voice piped up from the corner. At the same moment, the very girl in question melted into view.

"Don't get up," Samantha said quickly, teasingly polite, "and no powers either. We wouldn't want to have a repeat of our last little encounter, would we?"

Rae felt the blood drain from her head. The mirror reflection showed her very pale, and no matter how hard she tried she couldn't catch her breath. "Sam-mantha...how'd you get in here?"

Perhaps the better question would have been: how *long* have you been in here?

From the looks of things, it had been quite a while. There was a little stash of empty candy wrappers littering the floor around her, and judging by the heat rings on the table beside her she'd reheated the same cup of coffee almost a dozen times.

"Easy," she grinned, "I walked inside. You actually opened the door for me," she nodded her head at Gabriel, "but I asked you to forget the whole thing. The same way I asked all of you to simply *not see me* for..." she checked her watch, "the last few hours."

The second she said the words, she faded again from view. There was a collective gasp as the gang twisted around to find her, unable to leave their chairs. But less than a minute later, she popped back into sight. Giggling like a little kid.

"I wanted to listen in, you see." She kicked up her feet and set them on a nearby ottoman, completely ignoring the looks of shock and fury all around her. "I figured sooner or later you guys would figure out this whole thing was because of me. And then start working on one of your famous plans to bring me down." There was a strange giddiness about the way she said it. As if she had imagined being in the room for one of these legendary meetings many, many times before. "A girl's gotta protect herself by any means necessary." She shrugged and crossed her ankles. "Of course...I had no idea I'd be stumbling into the jackpot." She turned her taunting smile to Rae, freezing her there with her eyes. "Diving back into my past, making Julian bring it out into the future? That epic showdown with your dad?"

"You were there?" Devon asked through clenched teeth. "You saw all that?"

Samantha flashed him a bright smile, as brave as a girl at the zoo staring through the glass at a caged lion, unable to escape. "I sure did. It was some pretty cinematic stuff!"

Rae wondered if Samantha had been downstairs when she'd summoned the memory. Maybe Samantha had even held her hand so there was skin on skin contact. Rae couldn't remember, no matter how hard she tried.

"Then why do this?" Julian interjected, breaking Rae's thoughts. There was a dangerous glow to his eyes that the others rarely saw, a chilling malice that faded even Samantha's smile. "If this whole thing is about Simon, getting revenge for what he did, then why not kill him right there? We obviously couldn't have stopped you."

At this pronouncement, she leaned forward with sudden excitement. "Oh, because this isn't just about Simon anymore, is it?" Her eyes flickered around the circle, staring at each one of them in turn. "It's about all of you."

"Us?" Molly was the only one still struggling helplessly to get up from her chair, unable to take the confinement for even a second more. "Why the hell is it about us?"

As usual, Samantha was more than willing to share. "Because Simon's a monster." The word rang out true and clear around the room. No one would think to contest it. "He's evil to the core, and although he should be killed a thousand times over for what he's done—at this point—no one can realistically expect any different. But you?" Her eyes cooled, filling the others with sudden dread. "You should know better."

With that ominous declaration she slowly kicked back in her chair, staring around the room with dark anticipation. Paired with an equally dark smile.

"And I intend to teach you all that lesson, right now."

Chapter 11

"Let's begin, shall we?"

As far as super-villains went, talking with Samantha was nothing like conversing with Cromfield.

Rae almost laughed out loud at the comparison.

To start, Cromfield played the long game. Gabriel and Angel were living evidence of that. Every move was carefully calculated and planned years in advance. And no matter what cards he might be holding, there wasn't a chance in hell that he would ever show you a glimpse of his hand.

Samantha was different.

Call it a next-generation progression. Call it the arrogance of youth. Whatever the reason, the girl felt absolutely no need whatsoever to sensor herself. She lived moment to moment, making up the steps as she went along. Perfectly willing to tell anyone her master plan, simply because, even if they knew exactly what it was, there would be nothing they could do to stop it.

It was a point she was having the time of her life driving home.

"For starters, I think we should all get on the same page." Samantha leapt lightly from her chair, and began pacing in a little circle around the room, stopping occasionally to pause behind each of their chairs. Like a bizarre game of duck-duck-goose. *More like morbid*, Rae thought. "That way, I know what you're all thinking, you know what I'm thinking…" She flicked her wrist in the air. "It just makes the most sense moving forward. In fact," she came to a sudden stop, frozen between Luke and Molly, "I think from now on…*honesty* is our best policy."

At first, Rae could feel no change. Glancing around the room, she could tell the others were still waiting for it as well. But then, with a little prickling in the base of her skull, she began to feel it happening. It was like being drunk, but without the alcohol. That complete lack of censorship. An inability to mask even the most mundane details. No matter how hard she tried.

Rae's body fought it. Skipping through tatù after tatù to break the connection, and each time coming up empty-handed.

It was absolutely terrifying. To have one's entire life reduced to an open book. One just waiting for your greatest enemy in the world to pick up and read.

But Samantha had slightly different plans...

"Well," she clapped her hands, looking satisfied, "now that we got *that* behind us, I guess we should move on to the—"

"This is the girl?" Kraigan interrupted, staring Samantha up and down. He was strapped to his chair like the rest of them, unable to leave if his life depended on it. Yet there was still something very frightening in the way he spoke. The same way you wouldn't venture too close to a junkyard dog, regardless of the leash. "Doesn't look like much."

The others tensed, waiting for the fallout, but Samantha looked nothing short of delighted.

"You're the only one I haven't met yet." She skipped lightly across the room and came to a stop in front of his chair—safely out of arm's reach. "Kraigan, isn't it?"

He nodded curtly. Whether he wanted to or not.

"Tell me, Kraigan," she leaned an inch closer, her eyes dancing with wicked mischief, "since I didn't see you after the trial...where exactly did you go?"

He hesitated, bracing slightly against the chair. "I went..."

A wide smile stretched across her face as she leaned closer still.

"Come on," she said coaxingly, "tell me. I can keep a secret."

His eyes flashed pure murder, but he had no choice but to comply. "I went to my mother's grave," he said softly, tightly.

A surge of emotion welled up in Rae's heart as Samantha tilted her head back and laughed uproariously. Every part of her was aching to break free, aching to wipe that smirk off the kid's face once and for all. But the decision was no longer her own. Like an angry puppet, she could do nothing but sit there and watch, as deadly little Samantha played with the strings.

"You see, *that* is exactly what I don't understand." Her eyes danced as she returned to her chair, kicking back as if the two of them were chatting it up like old friends. "How the heck you could still love Simon even after what he did to your mother."

A feral growl shook Kraigan's shoulders. "You have no idea what he did."

"I know he didn't care about your mom," she replied bluntly. "I know she was just as expendable to him as my parents were. I know that Rae was born out of love, but you were nothing more than a sick little experiment." Kraigan's hands curled up into fists, but just as he opened his mouth with a furious reply she held up a hand. "*Don't* bother. I think we both know it's true."

Like someone was physically moving him, his mouth snapped shut. He glared at her with wild, unbridled rage but could do nothing more than sit.

"Samantha," Rae murmured desperately, "don't do this. You're angry with me. Not them. I'm the one who advocated for life. I'm the reason he's not dead."

Samantha slowly rotated around.

Rae gazed steadily back at her. "Let it be about me," she pressed. "Let the rest of them go. You can tell them to just walk away. Forget this ever happened. You know they'll do it. You know it's the right thing to do."

Samantha laughed humorlessly. "And when has a Kerrigan ever been concerned with doing the right thing?"

Rae reined in her frustration, trying her best to appear calm and reasonable. She'd spent most of her life trying to do the right thing. Samantha didn't get that. "You can still stop this—"

"And you're wrong again," Samantha interrupted. "This has never just been about you. The whole lot of you operate as a team. Everyone knows it. Unified decisions, and all that. Blah, blah, blah. That means that every time you do something crazy—like, say, keeping your murdering father alive—it's the rest of them who have to pay the price."

Rae fell silent, but it had nothing to do with Samantha. It was of her own accord.

It was a sore spot.

One that she dealt with all the time. One that she and the gang had discussed many, many times. They were always reassuring. She always terrified she was going to get them killed.

"No. Every person sitting here is just as responsible by now as you are." Samantha's eyes lit up with a sudden sparkle. "But I'd be willing to bet...that not all of them are as okay with that as they've led you to believe."

Like a kid in a candy store she rotated in a slow circle, looking at each one of them in turn.

Then she came to a sudden stop. "You don't see this as your fight at all, do you? In fact, I bet you resent the hell out of it."

There was a hitch in Angel's breathing and she cringed into her chair, refusing to acknowledge the question but unable to look away.

"You and your brother already won your fight," Samantha continued relentlessly. "You were born into terrible circumstances, like me, but fought your way free. This is supposed to be your clean slate. A fresh start. One that comes with an entire future." Her lips curled up in a knowing smirk. "But then came Rae."

Angel shifted nervously in her chair, her eyes flickering to Rae in spite of herself. "Rae comes with that future," she said evasively. "She's Julian's best friend."

Samantha shook her head, knowing Angel could only avoid the truth for so long. "She's the only thing standing *between* you two," she countered. "Between you and the life you've always wanted. Every time you think you've put it all behind you, Rae Kerrigan shows up with another hair-brained scheme and your boyfriend goes running after her."

Angel clenched her jaw, glaring with all her not-inconsiderable might. "It's not like that—"

"And you're forced to just follow along. Otherwise you'd get left behind. Otherwise Julian would have to choose between her and you, and you're not sure you want to know what he'd say."

"Rae didn't ask for her problems, and they're not limited to her alone," Angel fired back. "I may not agree with everything one hundred percent of the time, but she's just doing what she thinks is right. Even if—" She stopped cold, terrified of what she'd been about to say.

Samantha said it for her. "—Even if it's a huge mistake?"

A cold silence fell over the room.

Then Angel hung her head, and Samantha grinned.

"That's what I thought."

"That's enough!" Julian strained forward as far as he could manage, coming up just short of Angel's chair. "What the hell kind of game is this?! Angel and Gabriel have history with Simon that goes back even farther than yours. Of course you can't expect her to just jump on board—"

"Well, that's fairly predictable," Samantha silenced him with a teasing finger, pressing it up against his lips, "the boyfriend swoops in to the rescue. Always protecting her. Always saving." Her eyes danced with wicked excitement as she knelt in front of his chair. "But tell me, Julian...do you ever regret it?"

His handsome face froze as he tried to understand. "Regret it? Of course I don't—"

"What about that day on the bridge?"

There was a second of horrified silence, then Rae, Devon, and Molly started shouting at the same time. The specifics were lost in the profanities and clamor, but the gist of it was the same.

Samantha silenced them with a single hand; she didn't even glance their way. "I wasn't there, but I heard about it." Her eyes were shining, burning into his. "Two lives, in exchange for over a hundred? I don't care if they were on the wrong side or not. You can't tell me that you don't think about it. Wonder if you made the right call."

Julian's face went ghostly pale as he tried to keep himself together.

A silent tear ran down Rae's cheek; she quickly wiped it away. Thought about it? Yes, one could say that. He'd dreamt about it almost every night since it had happened. She and the others had heard him screaming in his sleep.

"It ended the fight," he murmured, fighting hard against her influence. "If I hadn't done it, Cromfield's followers would have won. Even more people would have died—"

"That sounds like a line one of the others gave you," Samantha cut him off. "Something they told you to help you sleep at night. But the fact remains: you traded the lives of you and your girlfriend for a hundred people you'll never know. So, my question is this: do you regret it?"

Don't—don't make him say it.

"I...I can't..."

Samantha twitched her fingers, and he winced in pain.

"Oooooh, I'm afraid you're going to have to," she carried on in a singsong voice. A voice that made Rae want to strangle her. "You were the one who made the trade. For the life of a girl you feel like you can't ever completely trust. The same girl who lied to you from the very beginning, who was reprogrammed to lack basic human emotions, who pulled out a knife just last week and stabbed someone right in front of you." Her voice rose slightly with each one, creating a wave. A wave designed to crush him. "For a girl you're afraid is just a little too twisted to ever fully love."

"That's not true! Those aren't my words," he cried. "Angel, you know that's not true!"

Samantha stepped in between them. Eyes dancing. Ready to deliver the final blow. She spoke slowly and carefully, letting her ink work its way deep into his mind. *"Do you ever regret it?"*

Julian fell silent, looking like he'd been punched in the face. Then his head bowed to his chest, and in a voice so soft they could barely hear it he dug his own grave. "...Yes," he whispered.

Another friend down.

Another bout of chilling laughter in its wake.

Rae ground her teeth together, clenching her armrests with all her might.

It was quickly becoming clear what Samantha's strategy was. It was as simple as it was devastatingly effective, given the truth-telling spell she'd placed over the room.

Why fight your enemies, when you can get them to fight each other?

"You bitch."

Samantha spun around to see Molly sitting rigid in her chair. Every line of her usually sunny face was set in hard anger, and the look in her eyes promised certain death were she ever set free.

"You think Simon Kerrigan was so terrible, but you're just like him." Her eyes flashed electric blue, hinting at sparks just below the surface. "Torturing people as part of some sick game."

They were bold words, and given Molly's present condition Rae would have given anything for her not to have said them. But she showed not an ounce of fear as Samantha walked her way.

"Torturing?" Samantha echoed innocently. "I'm not torturing anyone, Molly Skye. I'm *educating* you. You all came in here tonight hoping to plan my death. I'm simply showing you what you're up against. Reminding you that there's no reason to plan, because there's no way to fight."

To prove her point she snapped her fingers above her head, keeping her eyes locked on Molly the entire time.

There was a scrape of chairs as Angel and Luke pushed to their feet. Their eyes were just as blank as that day at Guilder, and there was a strange robotic quality to the way the moved.

Unfortunately, it was not enough to stop them.

They strode purposefully towards each other, and without a moment's hesitation they grabbed each other and began to kiss.

"Stop it!" Molly whispered, watching as Luke's hands wound through Angel's hair.

On the other side of the room Julian was staring with his mouth agape, as still as a statue.

"I said, stop it."

The kiss heated up. Hands were beginning to grope. Things rapidly picking up speed.

"STOP IT!"

Devon and Julian leapt to their feet at the same time, breaking through Samantha's command at the same time that Angel and Luke broke apart.

The forced couple stared at each other for a moment, confused as to how they'd gotten so close, before a sick kind of realization visibly settled upon their shoulders. Each one looked like they wanted nothing more than to bolt from the room, but the next second they were heading back to their chairs, marching as if invisible strings were pulling them along.

"I'd be careful," Samantha warned, swishing her skirt back and forth as she focused her attention on Devon and Julian who were still standing in the middle of the room. "Unless the two of you want to *really* get to know each other."

Both men paled and backed away but Samantha merely giggled, directing them with a wave of her hand to their seats. Her revenge may have been rooted in the deepest of hate, but it had become a game to her. One that there was no doubt in her mind she could win.

But there was one person who refused to play.

"Your father would be so proud."

A terrifying silence fell over the room as Samantha turned to Gabriel in what felt like slow motion.

He alone hadn't said anything since the minute they'd sat down. Since the minute they'd been frozen. He'd been watching instead. Studying his opponent. Planning his move.

Rae shook her head desperately as Samantha walked towards him, but he never broke eye contact. He just kept staring up at her with that calm self-assuredness. In fact, he was the only one besides Samantha herself who looked like he was completely at home.

"Look at what his little girl has become."

A hint of a snarl broke through Samantha's smug façade, and her fingers curled up into little fists. For a second the game fell away, and it looked like she was about to do away with him right then and there. As she stared down in the lamplight, Rae could swear she was actually debating it.

But it took an awful lot to scare a guy like Gabriel. As deadly as she may be, this little girl wasn't cutting it. And it had to be said, in all likelihood this wasn't the first time he'd been screwed around with in the head while tied to a chair.

"You speak so flippantly," she mused, almost to herself.

He smiled dryly. "I've been known to."

"You also speak as if you have an idea what you're talking about," she snapped. "But you don't. You have no idea what I've—"

"I have no idea what it's like to grow up without a father?" he interrupted caustically. "To have had some psychopath with a gun take him away? Really?" He shook his head. "Yeah, actually, I know a bit."

Samantha's eyes gleamed as she leaned forward, taking in every detail. "And yet you protect him."

"I'm not protecting him," Gabriel answered bluntly. "He's getting locked up for the rest of his life for what he's done."

She shook her head incredulously, looking as though she honestly didn't understand. "...You could have killed him."

Gabriel stared evenly at her, his face betraying not an ounce of emotion. "I considered it. I decided to do this instead."

With that, the tone of the conversation made an abrupt shift. Samantha crossed the room until she was standing right in front of him, relaxing her angry fists. There was an almost-hungry edge to the way she was looking at him now. A strange craving.

"You were always my favorite, you know?" Her eyes glowed wistfully as she looked him up and down, her eyes taking in every inch. "Whenever people would talk about you guys and the things you'd done...you were always the one I liked best."

Alicia had better stay far away. Otherwise Samantha might tell her to walk off a cliff.

For his part, Gabriel said nothing. He didn't even blink when she bent down and put her hands on his legs, leaning forward to whisper in his ear. "You have no idea the things I could do to you. The things I could make you do."

For a split second, Rae was terrified Samantha was about to show him. Burn it into their collective memory. She certainly looked ready to.

But Gabriel was unfazed. He simply shook back his golden hair, staring without concern at the far wall. "I'm sure you could make me do anything you want." He twisted his head slightly so they were face to face. And while she was the one who was technically calling the shots, it was his voice that somehow held all the power. "But then it's not really *me* doing it. It's you."

Her face darkened into a scowl as her cheeks reddened with a guilty flush. "Tell me, Gabriel, when you were working for the other side, how many times did you imagine seeing the people in this room dead? How many hybrids did you help Cromfield track down and kill? How many times, when you were trapped down in those caves, did you wish that Rae was the one in the ground—not you?"

The questions fired out like bullets, but Gabriel absorbed each one unflinchingly. Instead of looking angry or undone, his face grew momentarily thoughtful. "Every day of my life," he answered softly. "Every day of my life I wished for that."

Samantha paused. It was clearly not the answer she'd been expecting to hear. But bless his twisted heart, Gabriel wasn't nearly finished.

"But Rae knows that." The thoughtfulness was gone, replaced with a strength and certainty just as unyielding as Samantha's own. "I also used to be in love with her. She knows that, too." This time, it was he who leaned in, lowering his voice to the same theatric whisper. "I'm not playing this little game. *Honestly.*"

Samantha sprang back like she'd been burned, for the first time looking as though she wasn't entirely in control. Her eyes flickered back to Gabriel, but at this point he had her firmly in his sights, lounging back in the chair as though it was his idea to sit down in the first place.

"This was a bold move, sweetheart, but playtime's over." His green eyes burned into hers, cutting her down with every word. "You've overstayed your welcome. It's time to go home."

With a strange hiss, Samantha fell a step backward. Every ounce of curiosity and excitement melted from her face. Replaced with something cold. Something sour. "When this thing finally goes down," she growled, "count on me finding you."

Gabriel's lips twisted up in a cold smile, as lovely as it was lethal. "Honey, I wouldn't have it any other way."

Her eyes flashed, and with what looked like a great effort she forced herself to turn away from him—focusing her attention on the others instead. "On that very special day, I thought it best to even out the playing field. I know all about the PC's anklets and inhibitors. I'm sure that's what saved Simon that day by interfering with my ink." Her voice took on that supernatural persuasiveness. The tone that couldn't be ignored. "None of you will *ever* wear an inhibitor. *Never* put one on your skin. If someone else puts it there, you are to take it off at all costs. I don't care if it means cutting off your own leg."

The command was absorbed and set. Even though nothing had moved, even though nothing had outwardly changed, Rae was sure she would follow the order to the letter. Man, she wished she had Samantha's ink. Could she counter Samantha's commands?

"I really should be going now." Samantha crossed back to her chair and removed her coat, slipping it snugly over her shoulders. "I'm also going to have to ask you to wait a full minute or two after I leave the room before getting up. I have a bit of unfinished business with Simon Kerrigan that needs attending to. And on that note..." She suddenly spun around, fixing Rae in her sights. "I almost forgot to ask you my final question."

Rae braced in her chair, trying to act as brave as Gabriel. "What's that?"

Samantha's eyes glowed with a wicked smile. "After Devon stabbed you, when you were lying on the ground, bleeding out as you looked up at him...how did you feel?"

Even from across the room, Rae could hear the hitch in Devon's breathing. See how he psychologically fell apart, lost in the horror of the memory. But she stared straight up at Samantha. "I was afraid."

Of course she was. She didn't see the harm in admitting it. Didn't see the big surprise.

But leave it to Samantha to have something else up her sleeve.

The young girl nodded twice, frowning, as though she were a bit confused. Then she looked up at Rae with an innocent smile. A smile that seemed to grow stronger and stronger by the second. "And what about right now? No spells, no knives, sitting here in this room. When you look at Devon, when you stare into his eyes...how do you feel?"

Rae sucked in a quick breath as everything around her seemed to grow very still. She could not answer this question. She couldn't even lift her eyes.

But somehow, she had to. She had to do both.

The two of them locked eyes from across the room. Two people who knew each other as well as they knew themselves. Two people who loved each other more than anything in the world.

One was waiting breathlessly for the answer. The other was horrified to give it.

"...I feel afraid."

Chapter 12

And that ended the interrogation.

Samantha left a minute later, after making a quick stop in the basement to whisper some horrible nothing into Simon's ear. The others had stayed rooted to their chairs for exactly sixty seconds before springing in unison to their feet.

Kraigan rubbed his jaw painfully, finally able to open it. Angel took one look at Julian and headed upstairs without a word. Devon took one sad look at Rae, then sank back into his chair. Molly took one glance at Luke and crossed her arms protectively over her belly.

"Molls...?" he began tentatively, looking terrified to approach her. "Babe, I'm so sorry. I didn't mean to. I didn't even know what was happening until it was all done."

Molly jerked her head up and down very quickly. There were tears in her eyes, but they refused to fall. And when she was finally able to speak, it was in a voice much higher than her own. "I'm...I'm going to sleep in Rae's room tonight."

Rae glanced over in surprise, but instantly nodded her agreement. By the looks of things, she and Devon certainly weren't going to be sleeping in the same bed.

Luke, on the other hand, looked absolutely crushed. His blue eyes tightened painfully, but before he could say anything Molly held up her hands.

"I'm not mad or anything, I swear. I just...I need a night. Okay?"

He stared at her for a second, then bowed his head. "Of course. Whatever...whatever you want."

The two of them disappeared a second later, heading in opposite directions when they reached the top of the stairs. The rest of the gang stared after them for a second, then Gabriel slowly pushed to his feet. He nodded a curt goodnight, but before he could leave Rae stopped him.

"How did you do that? With Samantha?" She didn't want to ask, she didn't want to even think about it...but she had to know. "How did you know what to do?"

Gabriel was quiet for a second, lost in thought. Then he flashed her a sad smile. "Cromfield liked to play games." He left without another word, pausing in the doorway as he passed Julian. The psychic tensed, bracing as if he was about to get hit. But Gabriel clapped him on the shoulder instead, then vanished up the darkened stairway after his sister.

In the end, it was just Rae and Kraigan across from Julian and Devon. None of them knew what to say. None of them even knew where to start.

Finally, after several long minutes, Julian broke the silence.

"How do I fix this?" he murmured, still staring at the spot where Angel had disappeared into the darkness. "She's never going to speak to me again."

Devon glanced at him, but his usual words of advice failed him. Instead, he merely bowed his head, taking great care not to look at his fiancée who was also standing in the dark. "I don't know if you can," he answered softly. "I don't know if there's any fixing this."

Rae sucked in a silent breath. His words weren't just for Julian; they were for her as well. And as much as she wanted to scream them down, as much as she wanted to blanket the room in refusals and denials, she didn't know if she could do that.

Because she didn't know if they were true.

"I'm going to check on Simon," she said flatly, deciding to excuse herself altogether. "Find out what Samantha did to him before I get to bed."

Devon was silent. Julian was silent.

In the end, it was Kraigan who spoke up. "Good idea. I'll go with you."

Together, the two of them separated from the others and made their way down the hall to the basement. Rae wondered how Samantha knew so much about them, how she had figured out all their weaknesses. It was crazy. She sighed, almost thankful she didn't have Samantha's power. As she looked around, Rae was becoming hyper-aware of the fact that the entire house had been divided into sections. That the lines between them had started to splinter and split.

But that was a problem for tomorrow. Enough had happened today. Today needed to end.

Simon was standing in the middle of the basement when they got there. From a distance he didn't look to be harmed, but Rae had long ago learned not to be deceived by appearances. She and Kraigan made their way down the stairs slowly, carefully. Well aware that, at any moment, their father was likely to strike.

Except he didn't strike. He smiled instead.

"There they are!" He opened his arms wide, grabbing his children in a crushing embrace. "My pride and joy. My true legacy."

Kraigan and Rae exchanged an incredulous look behind Simon's back as he squeezed the life out of them, turning his head to kiss them both on the cheek.

"You know, I have to admit I didn't think that I'd ever see the two of you standing in the same room. I'd planned on keeping you secret from each other forever." His face cracked into a beaming smile, delighted to have been proven wrong. "Isn't it strange how things work out?"

As Kraigan stared back at him in shock, Rae shut her eyes with a painful grimace.

Great, just great.

It looked like Samantha had given dear ol' dad a bit of her magic truth serum as well...

The sleeping arrangements that night were like a game of musical chairs.

Molly slept in Rae's room. Gabriel slept on the floor in Angel's. Kraigan haunted his little cot up in the attic like usual, while Luke, Julian, and Devon passed out in the living room. For his part, Simon had been given a room at the far end of the hall. This was only after Rae had asked him point blank if he intended to either run, hurt them, or steal any of their powers. When he'd replied in the negative to all three with a supernaturally-persuaded smile, she unlocked the basement door.

The last thing she wanted to do was show him even an extra modicum of kindness but, to be frank, she didn't see any other way to get out of that unexpected family hug. She was just thankful her mother wasn't in the place to witness it.

The house went quiet the second the lights went out but, try as she might, Rae was unable to sleep. And it wasn't the residual adrenaline from Samantha's psychological attack. It wasn't even the constant barrage of sharp little sleep kicks coming from Molly's side of the bed.

It was the look on Devon's face the second she'd said she was afraid.

To Samantha's credit, Rae didn't think there was a single worse question in the entire world for her to force Rae to answer. No deadlier weapon she could have used. There was no hope, determination, or life left on his face when it was done. It was a barb that went straight to his heart.

All from a little word...*afraid*.

Is it really true? Rae wondered as she dodged another of Molly's midnight kicks. *Am I really still afraid of him?*

She certainly didn't feel afraid of him. When she looked at his face she didn't find herself worried, or uneasy, or uncertain as to what he might do. She didn't automatically reposition herself whenever he walked into a room—making sure there was a protective distance, or barrier between them at all times. If anything, it was exactly the opposite.

She was the one who'd reached for him, still declaring her love, even as he walked towards her with the knife. She was the one who stopped him from leaving. The one who'd grabbed his hands and forced him to get over his own fears. Forced him to stay.

So how could I still be afraid of him?

If it wasn't for the fact that Samantha's command for honesty had triggered the answer, Rae wouldn't have believed it herself. But ink like that wasn't something you could get away from. Any more than Julian admitting he sometimes wondered if he'd made the right choice, saving his and his girlfriend's life. Any more than Luke kissing Angel. Than Kraigan's forced silence. Than all of them cemented to their chairs. The ink was sound, and that meant only one thing.

If Rae had said she was afraid…that meant it must be true.

Another fitful kick caught her right in the stomach, and she slipped out of bed with a quiet sigh. Sleep was impossible and she couldn't stand to be in that room for another minute. The room that she and Devon were supposed to be sharing. The room they slept in together.

Quieter than a ghost, she padded down the hall and made her way to the kitchen. All the lights were out, and the sound of deep breathing whispered from the living room where the boys were sleeping. She cast them a quick glance before slipping into her fiancé's tatù. The last thing she wanted to do was startle them awake. After the evening they'd had with Samantha, she was surprised they were able to fall asleep in the first place.

As it turned out, not everyone was so lucky…

Chapter 13

"Hey."

Rae whipped around to see that she wasn't the only one prowling around the house in the middle of the night. Devon was standing by the cupboards in his pajama bottoms and white top; a mug of hot chocolate in one hand, a bottle of peppermint schnapps in the other.

It had to be said, even after everything that had happened that night, he still looked utterly adorable. Hot, sexy, and everything that she fell in love with during her first year at Guilder. His dark hair was curly in some parts and pointy in others—like he'd been tossing and turning just as much as Rae. It was that delicious length that made her swoon, but his mother would surely insist he trim. His shirt was rumpled and clung to him like a second skin, discreetly hinting at the sculpted muscles hiding just beneath. And his eyes, while bright as ever, were dilated almost entirely black under the light of the full moon.

Rae pursed her lips, trying to stifle a smile. "Your shirt's on backwards."

He glanced down at his chest in surprise before flashing her a rueful grin. "I can't believe I just fell for that."

She grinned back. "It must be the schnapps."

He waved the bottle in the air before adding a splash to his hot chocolate. It smelled festive and delicious, perking Rae up even across the room. "It's the one good thing Angel brought with her when she moved in." He gestured invitingly to the cupboard and Rae nodded. He got her a mug. "She said, 'posh boys shouldn't be so wound up.' That we needed to relax a little. This helped."

Rae laughed quietly as he mixed the ingredients and then slid the mug across the counter. "*Posh* boys?" she repeated.

Devon shook his head. "Her words, not mine. I guess it's all relative, you know? Not all of us could grow up beneath a cemetery."

Rae laughed again and took a sip. It was good. Better than good, in fact. She sensed a middle of the night tradition starting. "Do you ever miss that house?"

The question came out of nowhere, surprising them both. It was remarkably mundane, given the things they usually were forced to talk about, but was layered with implication nonetheless. Even so, the mundane helped. They needed a little normalcy after a day like this. The second he finished answering, she full intended to ask him about the weather.

Devon pulled in a deep breath and hopped lightly upon the counter, never spilling a drop. "Sure. It's a great house." He paused, thinking back with a faint grin. "Granted, it was never supposed to be me, Julian, and Angel living in it. It wasn't even supposed to be me and Jules—not for much longer. It was always supposed to be me and you."

Rae dropped her eyes and nodded. She remembered the night well. The night that Devon had bought the house and led her through the park to see it. At first, she hadn't understood. It was absolutely lovely. Ivy climbing up the walls. Flowers planted in the front. Even the thick, double-paned windows. Every single thing about it was perfect.

Except...Devon *bought* a house?

That's when he told her why he did it. That's when he told her who the house was really for.

It had been the first time they'd talked so openly about their future. Not just whimsical hypotheticals and broad declarations of love. But in concrete, logistical terms. Terms that, while lacking the poetry of some of their speeches, still managed to sweep her off her feet.

He wanted to put down roots with her, he'd said. Wanted to build a life together. No matter how strange it might be. No matter if they were always reaching for 'normal,' that proverbial white unicorn dancing just out of sight. They would do it together. Every step—together.

Because they loved each other. Because they didn't need anything more.

"I've always loved that robe on you."

Rae looked up in surprise. She hadn't heard him move, but he was suddenly standing right in front of her. The sound of his soft voice brought her out of her nostalgic trance.

"What—this?" She looked down in confusion, a little embarrassed at the same time. It wasn't exactly what she'd call the sexiest thing in her wardrobe. Quite the contrary. The thick navy terrycloth and bright spattering of stars would have looked more at home at a junior high slumber party. Over the years, Molly had tried several times to 'accidentally' set it on fire, but Rae had rescued it every time. "That...doesn't seem likely." She glanced up doubtfully, but Devon was staring down with a tender smile.

His hands came up tentatively to slip under the belt loops, gently pulling her closer. "Well, I happen to have several fond memories...of taking it off you."

Even in the dark, she could see his dimples.

An automatic blush colored her cheeks as she bit down on her lip with a smile. She was thrilled by the proximity, but even more, she was thrilled that he was the one initiating it. That he wasn't so demoralized by what she'd been forced to admit that he was keeping his distance. "Devon, I—"

His lips came down over hers, stealing her breath as his hands wound back through her long hair. No matter how close he was, it was like he couldn't get close enough. The mugs of schnapps were pushed aside and forgotten as his arms wrapped tentatively around her back, squeezing her against his chest as tightly as he dared.

Rae gasped just once in surprise, then closed her eyes and embraced it wholeheartedly. The second she'd seen him standing in the kitchen, she'd started gearing up for painful discussion. For an emotionally-dense heart-to-heart, one which would surely leave them both feeling more confused than ever by the time they walked away.

She hadn't been expecting this.

"Dev," she whispered again, smiling as he abandoned her lips and began trailing feather-light kisses down her neck, "anyone could just walk in—"

"We'd hear them coming," he murmured. In an act of sheer recklessness his fingers slipped beneath her shirt, leaving a trail of goosebumps on everything they touched. "We'll be fine."

She let out a soft moan and, without thinking grabbed the collar of his shirt, yanking him closer so they could kiss once more. Things got more heated after that. In a blur of speed, he picked her up and set her down on the counter. Her legs wrapped around his waist of their own accord, and before she knew what was happening he peeled off his shirt and dropped it on the floor.

Um—WOW.

For a second, she allowed herself to simply stare. Unabashedly running her eyes up and down his flawless body. Unable to believe how this man was possibly hers.

This is a public kitchen.

"Dev," she tried again, hyper-aware of the two boys still sleeping in the next room, "we should really—"

Another silencing kiss. Followed by a hundred more.

"It's going to be fine." His breath quickened as he started fiddling with the drawstring on her pants. "I promise."

There was an urgency now to the way he moved. A strange kind of desperation that filled Rae with a quiet panic. Hands gripping manically around her own. Pounding, uneven pulse.

This wasn't Devon. Devon wasn't a sex-on-countertops kind of guy. At least, not when his best friend was a stone's throw away. There was something else behind this. Something not good.

"Dev, I'm serious. Wait."

He pulled back immediately, the second he registered the shift in her tone. A rush of cool air swept between them, and Rae's mind raced as she struggled to think of what to say.

But as it turned out...the next line wasn't hers.

"Please..."

She looked up in shock, only to have that shock double when she saw the look on Devon's face. Long gone was the cool confidence. Long gone was the winking sex appeal that had gotten her up on the counter in the first place. The man standing in front of her looked... scared.

"Devon?" she whispered, eyes widening in the dark. "What is it?"

Despite everything they'd been through, she could count on one hand the number of times she'd ever seen him scared. It didn't come easy to him, and never once had it been for himself. Each time it had been for someone he loved. Most times, it was for her.

But he was scared now. So scared he could hardly speak.

"Please don't be afraid of me."

And just like that she suddenly understood. Understood the flood of emotions that had been coursing through her since the moment Samantha left. Understood the answer to that terrible question that had been tearing them both apart.

Without making a sound, she hopped off the counter and came to stand right in front of him. His entire body braced as she gazed up into his eyes, terrified to look. Terrified to look away.

"I am afraid," she whispered. "Samantha was right. When I look at you, I'm afraid. But Devon..." she pressed her lips together a moment, "it's not for the reason you think." Her hand slipped into his, and he actually stopped breathing. "I'm afraid to lose you."

The second she said the words, they were so obvious. Like they'd been there all along.

Of course she wasn't actually frightened of Devon himself. The man was in love with her, had asked her to be his wife. Had jumped off a cliff just to save her life. There was no one she feared less. There was no one she trusted more. But she was frightened of what Devon could do to her. Of the power he held. Not over her body, but over her heart.

She was terrified of what would happen if she ever lost him.

"When we were first dating, you broke up with me to protect me from our laws. When we were battling Cromfield you almost killed yourself with a serum, trying to keep me safe." Her voice was a low, practiced murmur. One that wouldn't carry to anyone farther than him. "After you stabbed me, your first thought was to isolate yourself." She pulled in a deep breath, forcing herself to finish. "And now Samantha..."

She couldn't finish after all. But she didn't need to. He understood what she couldn't say.

For a moment, neither one of them said anything. His eyes were fixed on her, while hers were fixed on the floor. Then, when it could go on no longer, he cleared his throat. "Is that really true?" He was being cautious, not daring to let himself believe. "Is that it? The thing you've been afraid of? It's not...it's not *me*?"

Rae's face melted into a warm smile, one that lit her from the inside. "Sweetheart, I hate to break it to you but you're not all that scary."

With a gasp of laughter he scooped her up into the air, hugging her against his chest with enough force to crush a regular person. Her body switched automatically into a strength tatù to protect itself as her arms wrapped around his neck.

"I love you, Devon Wardell." She flicked back a lock of his messy hair, and kissed him softly on the lips. "Nothing will ever change that. For better or worse. Forever and ever."

His heart quickened as his lips curved up in a breathtaking smile. "I'm going to hold you to that, you know."

She leapt lightly from his arms, landing on the floor with a grin. "You do that. But in the meantime," she reached out coyly and took his hand, "I've lost all interest in hot chocolate, and the entire house is still asleep."

He cocked his head to the side, staring at her quizzically. "What does that—"

She pressed a finger over his lips with a little grin, and started leading him out of the kitchen. "There's an empty room at the end of the hall..."

Chapter 14

As it turned out...there was *not* an empty room at the end of the hall.

The empty room had been given to Simon just a few hours earlier. It was a fact that Rae remembered just as she and Devon stumbled inside, lost in the process of tearing off what was left of each other's clothes. It was a close call, and if it wasn't for the fact that the young couple was equipped with superpowers, it could have been an even closer call than it was.

That being said, it was only after Rae raced back upstairs, slumping in mortification against her bedroom door, that she remembered her father was equipped with the exact same power.

That was the thought looping through her head the next morning when she headed down the stairs to get some breakfast. Molly and Luke were already sitting at the kitchen table, foreheads touching as they carried on a murmured conversation with a smile. Gabriel was standing by the far wall, arms folded across his chest as he stared fixedly out the window. And Simon was standing on the other side of the room, sipping from a cup of coffee.

He looked up as Rae breezed inside, flashing her a wry smile. "Morning, sunshine. You sleep okay?"

There was a hitch in her breathing, and even equipped with Devon's graceful tatù she still managed to spill boiling coffee all over her hands. "Ouch!" She leapt backwards, waving her scalded fingers in the air. "Uh...yeah, I slept fine. Me and Molly bunked together," she added quickly.

For the last time, apparently.

Rae wasn't sure when exactly it had happened, but it was obvious that Luke and Molly had gotten past the strange tension of the other night. Her legs were swung across his, and the two were laughing quietly as he absentmindedly buttered her toast. Every now and then, he would reach a hand down to touch her belly.

She did, however, look up when she heard her name.

"Kerrigan, you are the world's biggest klutz." Molly's blue eyes twinkled with amusement as she gazed across the kitchen at her best friend's scorched hands. "Bet you wish Alicia was here right now; she could take care of those burns."

"Bet you wish Alicia was here right now, too," Luke added slyly, glancing at Gabriel.

Gabriel flipped him off, but never took his eyes off the window.

"What burns?" Devon breezed into the kitchen, looking surprisingly well-rested considering his late-night dalliance over schnapps. His eyes tightened with concern when he saw Rae's hands, and before she could stop him he swept towards her, smoothing them flat in his palms. "Babe, what happened? Tell me this wasn't another failed attempt at making toast..." He trailed off upon seeing the pointed look on her face, and followed her gaze to where her father was standing—arms crossed—just behind his shoulder. A good deal of color drained out of his face, and although he kept his voice remarkably calm he dropped her hands at once. "Good morning, Simon."

His polite smile went unreciprocated as Simon stared back with a chilling expression Rae could only describe as '*Dad.*' An expression made all the worse when that dad was Simon Kerrigan.

"Is it?"

Devon gulped and retreated to the other side of the room, joining Gabriel in his vigil at the window.

Rae was quick to follow, avoiding her father's eyes as she skirted around the counter. "What are you even looking at out here?" she asked, worming her way in between the two men. "It better not be another...*oh*—that doesn't look good."

Julian and Angel were standing at the edge of the tree-line, having what looked to be the fight of a lifetime.

One was rooted to the spot, clearly trying to rein in his temper, while the other paced around like an angry little storm cloud, periodically throwing back her waves of ivory hair. Even so far away, the others could still hear the rise and fall of angry voices, and whenever there was a temporary lull Angel would jam an accusatory finger at his chest, and the whole thing would start up again.

At one point Julian threw up his hands in exasperation, yelling something that—even all the way back at the house—sounded like a very bad word. Even the coffee maker fell silent.

Coincidentally, that was the same point at which Rae decided to switch out of Devon's tatù.

Devon, who didn't have that luxury, leaned away from the window with a sympathetic wince. "They don't do things halfway, do they?"

"It's a *passionate* relationship," Molly piped up from the kitchen table. She had worked so hard for so long to insert herself into Julian's love life, she felt quite entitled to comment upon it now. "And you know what they say: the hotter the fights, the hotter the..." She trailed off as five sets of eyes turned her way. "Uh...never mind."

Rae and Devon returned to the window with various degrees of amusement. Gabriel, on the other hand, looked rather sick. But there was a chance that Molly was on the right track.

As quickly as it started, it seemed the fight was suddenly winding down. The pacing stopped, the voices quieted, and a second later Julian pulled Angel into his arms.

She slapped him. Then she kissed him.

Then she slapped him once more and headed inside.

Passionate indeed.

"That girl is freaking crazy..." Devon murmured incredulously as she marched back across the grass.

"Careful," Gabriel warned, although it looked like he didn't entirely disagree.

The three of them leapt away from the window the second they heard the door, settling around the table as innocently as could be.

But Angel was in no way fooled.

"Eavesdroppers go to hell, you know," she snapped before she grabbed her brother's cup of coffee and stormed away upstairs.

Her boyfriend came in next, looking decidedly more subdued.

Devon sprang to his feet. "Hey, man, you okay?"

"Yeah," Julian answered, looking only slightly whiplashed, "fine."

Gabriel grinned and handed him a cup of coffee. "Hang in there, kid."

Rae bit her lip, still feeling decidedly sorry for herself given her late-night mishap with her father, but flashed him a look of support.

Molly, on the other hand, was insufferably invested. "Do you want to talk about it?" she asked hopefully, patting the seat beside her. "And before you give me the same answer you always do, just keep in mind that I'm your best friend, I'm a spectacular listener and, to be honest, I'm basically the one who got you and Angel together in the first place. So, it's kind of my right to know."

Simon lifted his eyebrows, clearly amused with the way she didn't need to breathe. But the others had long-since grown accustom to such a rant. They averted their gaze with identical smiles, while Julian shook his head with a weary sigh.

"For the last time, Molls. You did not get Angel and me together. We met in Florence; you were in an entirely different country."

"Yeah, but what about in San Francisco?" she insisted.

He paused. "What *about* in San Francisco?"

"You remember!" Her eyes lit up with a nostalgic smile. "That time when I encouraged you to sneak us all into her apartment on a fake booty call, so that we could torture her for information!"

Julian blinked in disbelief as Luke slowly lowered his face into his hands.

Molly remained oblivious, rewarding each of them with a triumphant smirk. "If that's not good matchmaking, I don't know what is."

In perhaps the greatest timing in the world, the front door opened again and the gang was spared from having to answer.

There was a sound of quiet voices, then Beth raised her voice. "Hello, hello! Where is everyone?"

Rae rose quickly to her feet, giving Julian a sympathetic pat as she did. "We're in the kitchen, Mom!"

Her mother had gone back to Guilder the previous day, along with Keene and Fodder, to survey the damage incurred after the trial. It was another bout of brilliant timing in that she had missed Samantha's little visit entirely. Rae saw this as a blessing. Beth would not.

"It's freezing out there," Beth said as she joined them in the kitchen, sliding off her long trench coat and tossing it over the counter. "It has to only be about..." She trailed off suddenly as she saw Simon.

It was an abruptly awkward moment. Especially considering the way he was following her every move. Especially since the last time they saw each other he was holding her in his arms.

Beth did her best to recover, but the shock of rounding a corner and seeing her resurrected husband had yet to fade. And he certainly wasn't making it easy. Not with the way he was staring.

"Did you want to say something, Kerrigan?" she snapped.

His eyes sparkled as he stared at her with a tender smile. "You are as beautiful as the first day I met you."

Okay... *Now* it was an awkward moment.

Beth froze, while Fodder, who had just walked in behind her, lifted his eyebrows in surprise.

Rae, on the other hand, rushed forward, wondering if it was possible to both faint and throw up at the same time. "He didn't mean that! He's under a sort of spell!"

Fodder turned his look of surprise to her, but Beth couldn't stop staring at Simon.

"A spell?" she said, keeping him warily in her gaze. "What kind of spell?"

Rae's heart fluttered with increasingly nervous energy, and she glanced back at her friends for help. A row of silent, unhelpful faces stared back at her.

No. They were not getting in the middle of a Kerrigan-marriage dispute. Tough luck, Rae.

"It was...it's Samantha's tatù—spell—whatever you call it, actually." Rae closed her eyes and braced for the explosion. She was not disappointed.

"WHAT?!" Beth screamed. "You saw her AGAIN?! She came to the HOUSE?!"

It was amazing how much each of those words could resonate in the little kitchen.

Rae flinched and nodded, feeling strangely guilty for the whole thing. Probably because she had forgotten to call afterwards. It was a hard instinct to learn, after getting by alone for so long. On Beth's other side, Fodder was glaring daggers at his youngest son. *That* explosion would come later. "The group of us sat down in the living room for a little...talk," Rae edited carefully. Best not to tell her about the confinement. Or the threats. Or the impromptu make-out session there at the end. "But she forced us all to do so honestly. Every word we said was the absolute truth." She cast an apologetic glance at her father. "We were all released from it after she left. Apparently...apparently Simon wasn't."

It was a rather brilliant move on Samantha's part, Rae had to admit. If there was one way to turn the world against Simon Kerrigan, it was to force him to tell the truth.

That being said, Simon didn't seem to mind. In fact, he was still looking at Beth as if the last fifteen years had never happened. As if they were just teenagers at Guilder again, training together in the Oratory as they fell more and more in love.

"Would you like some coffee, my dear?" He pulled down a mug from the cupboard, glancing over his shoulder with a smile. "Still take it black with two sugars?"

Okay, this is WAY too weird...

"How did it go with you guys?" Rae asked quickly, changing the subject. "Did you and Keene get a chance to talk about what comes next?"

As President of the Privy Council, she was automatically at the head of any decision-making process. But as the daughter of the accused, the matter had been passed along to less-biased hands.

"We did, actually." Fodder stepped forward, graciously relieving Beth from the spotlight in light of weightier things. "And I think you'll find it a bit of a surprise."

That doesn't sound good...

"In light of the present threat from Miss Neilson, and taking into account the extreme measures Mr. Kerrigan took to save the lives of those gathered at the assembly...the Council has decided to temporarily suspend his sentence."

Rae stared at him in shock, unable to believe it was true.

They were suspending Simon's sentence? After everything she'd seen? After everything he'd done? How was it possible that they would just look the other way?

"This is only a temporary measure," Fodder reassured her, guessing her thoughts. He, too, had taken the journey back into the horrors of Simon's past. He did not take it lightly. "Provisional supervision, just until the culprit is found. Until she is, we simply cannot risk transporting him to a detention center."

"Why not?" Luke asked incredulously. "It's a simple enough task."

"Simple enough, perhaps, but a dangerous one as well." Fodder's eyes rested lightly upon his son. "To start, we would have no idea of knowing if she was already inside."

As the rest of them fell silent, considering all the implications of such a power, Rae started to put two and two together. Provisional supervision? Surely that couldn't mean—

"Here?" She interrupted the quiet discussions around her, zeroing in on Fodder with her arms folded over her chest. "You want him to stay here? *Again*?"

"Oh, Rae, isn't it wonderful?" Simon's eyes glowed as he looked between his estranged wife and his daughter. "The entire family under the same roof."

Rae stifled a gag as Beth turned sharply on her heel and walked out of the room. Leaving it to Fodder to work out the rest of the details she hurried after her, catching up by the front door.

"Mom!" she called, skidding to a stop beside her on the tile. Beth paused, and gave her a moment to catch her breath. "Mom...I'm really sorry about not calling about Samantha. It happened really late at night, and we all just got up. It wasn't really—"

"Honey, I'm not mad at you about Samantha. With everything else that's going on," she paused as her eyes flickered reflexively back to the kitchen, "I can see how it slipped your mind."

Rae followed her gaze, then turned back with a worried expression. "Are you going to be...*okay*, with this?" She bit her lip, uncertain exactly how to continue. "I know it's a lot to ask..."

Much to her surprise, Beth threw back her head with a laugh. "A lot to ask? Being trapped inside a mansion with my recently *un*-deceased husband? All I'd need for it to get really weird is a supernatural truth serum thrown on top."

Rae nodded quickly, pursing her lips. "Yeah, that was a stupid question."

Beth's hand slipped into hers. "It wasn't a stupid question. It was sweet. And it's not you who's asking. It's the Council, and the Knights, and a whole lot of other people who are afraid and need some kind of reassurance." She glanced back at the kitchen again, this time with a little sigh. "If we can help give them that by keeping an eye on him...then, yes. I can learn to be *okay* with it."

The two women stood there, side by side, as a voice echoed up from the kitchen.

"We should see if Kraigan's awake yet." Simon sounded nothing short of delighted by the whole idea. "Maybe the four of us could have lunch...?"

Rae shot a sideways glance at her mother, who closed her eyes with a painful sigh.

"But that doesn't mean I have to like it."

Chapter 15

"Attention, shoppers: to the person using laundry detergent to make a slip-and-slide on aisle seven, please stop."

Rae and her friends paused for a moment, gazing up towards the ceiling, before shrugging it off and making their way further into the store.

In an effort to escape the sudden awkwardness brought about by a newly-liberated and oh-so-honest Simon, Rae and Molly had decided to run out to the local grocery store to buy ingredients for dinner. Neither one of them had any experience cooking, of course, but between one's natural over-abundance of enthusiasm and the other's burning desire to escape her father—it had only taken a minute for them to convince themselves that it was a tremendous idea.

Devon and Luke, appalled to be left behind, had instantly jumped on board. Prompting Julian and Angel to feel left out. Prompting Gabriel to get dragged along. Prompting Kraigan to get paranoid they were plotting against him, so he tagged along as well.

In the end, all eight of them had ended up cramming into a trio of sports cars and heading into town. They'd parked in a little row near the back of the lot so as not to draw attention, but what with the rather ostentatious nature of the cars in question—along with a set of diplomatic flags that Rae had gotten from the Future Queen of England as a birthday gift—they tended to stand out.

No more so than their drivers.

Rae stifled a smile as a girl, who looked to be about her age, stared at Devon long enough that she accidently rammed her cart into a wall. She was in good company. The floor was still littered with fallen apples from when a man had done the exact same thing upon seeing Angel.

"Do you think that was real?" Luke asked, still hung up on the intercom. "A slip-and-slide?"

Kraigan's eyes lit up in a rare moment of excitement. "Only one way to find out..."

The next second the two of them took off, leaving the others behind.

"Hey!" Molly called after them. "*Hey*! Would you guys stop being silly? We came here for a reason, you know!"

Luke pretended not to have heard as he and Kraigan slipped around a corner and out of sight. Molly glared after them for a second before pushing the cart on with a self-righteous sigh. "Honestly, sometimes I think he needs a sitter," she huffed, browsing without any clear agenda through a selection of breakfast cereals. "The guy spends half his life working for an elite, covert agency trying to keep the world afloat, but the second you remove the pressure it's like he reverts back to freaking preschool."

Rae glanced over her shoulder to where Devon and Julian were fencing each other with a pair of salad tongs. "Must be a man thing..."

"Hey," Gabriel interjected, "you don't see me—*oh*, Molly, get that one." He pointed eagerly to the box she was still holding in her hand. "That's the one with the decoder ring."

The girls gave him a long look before slowly pushing the cart forward.

"Do you think this is what it would be like?" Molly mused, placing the cereal in the cart anyway as they wandered further up the aisle. "If none of this craziness was happening right now? If things were just..."

Rae caught the wistful note in her voice, and finished the question with a knowing smile. "Normal?"

Molly met her gaze before glancing down in spite of herself at her flat stomach. "Yeah...normal."

Both girls went quiet for a moment, lost in thought, before they were interrupted by the third, and predictably eccentric, member of their feminine trio.

"In my experience, there is no such thing as *normal*." Angel skipped out ahead of them, happily sporting her chef's hat. When she'd found out this was a trip to facilitate 'cooking dinner,' she'd whipped the thing out so fast Rae could have sworn she conjured it. Since then, she'd been vacillating between extreme interest and extreme boredom. Alternatingly either sticking random items in the cart, or napping curled up inside. "There's just whatever present reality your day happens to include," she continued. "If there's something more normal out there, I certainly haven't found it."

With that bit of unexpected wisdom she was off, springing lightly down the aisle in the hunt for her next entertainment.

Molly and Rae stared after her with wide eyes. It didn't happen often, the girl knew how to hide it well, but every now and then the others got a glimpse of that magic that Julian saw every day. The same magic that had made him fall in love with her.

That being said...she didn't exactly make things easy.

"You'd think she'd never been inside a grocery store before," Molly murmured, watching as Angel seized upon the notion of 'pasta' with a fervor, and began piling it up in her arms.

"She hasn't," Gabriel replied distractedly. When the two girls looked up in astonishment, he offered them a simple shrug. "She grew up beneath a church and spent her only years above ground living off take-out while trying to seduce your clairvoyant best friend. When would she have possibly gone to a grocery store?"

It was sound logic, and yet...

Rae took over pushing the cart with a little sigh. "Maybe Angel's right. Maybe there is no normal."

They wandered on for the next several minutes, listening with increasing entertainment as it became clear that Luke and Kraigan had effectively hijacked the intercom.

"Attention shoppers: Beware of the loose wolverine in the produce department."

"So, what is it exactly that you ladies are making?" Gabriel eyed the odd assortment of items in the cart with an amused smile. "So far it looks like beef broth and...toys."

Unfortunately, the grocery store had actually turned out to be one of those super-stores that had a little bit of everything. With so many options, the girls had found themselves ironically stuck.

"And an apple," Rae added indignantly.

"Yeah," Molly pointed defensively behind her back, "you missed the apple!"

"Rabies vaccines are available at customer service."

"You're right, how could I have possible missed the apple?"

"You know what, Alden?" Rae folded her arms across her chest. "I'm getting pretty freakin' tired of you lashing out with these random criticisms, based on nothing but—"

"—but fact?" Gabriel finished with a raised eyebrow.

Molly bristled defensively, stuffing her hands in her jacket pockets as the tips of them began to glow. "No one asked for your opinion, you know. You should take a page from the rest of the guys, and go busy yourself doing something useful."

"First one to find the lucky carrot wins a prize."

The four of them blinked, then stared purposely in opposite directions.

"You know what, you're right." Gabriel pursed his lips as he backed out of the aisle, making a bee-line for the liquor. "I think I will go do something useful."

"Fine."

"Go."

"No one cares."

The three girls waved him off, then turned back to their cart in wilted defeat.

"I guess we didn't really decide what we were going to be making," Rae muttered.

Angel's sapphire eyes narrowed as they scanned the collection. "What about cereal?"

"For dinner?" Molly crossed her arms over her chest. "You want to have cereal for dinner?"

Rae bit her lip, caught between the two of them. "It might be the only thing we can successfully cook, Molls."

"No, no. Not a chance." Molly straightened up to her full height, brimming with fresh determination as she took off down the next aisle. "I'm growing a tiny person over here. I need balanced meals, otherwise the thing will be born with gills or something. *Nutritious* dinners."

Angel considered this for a moment before her face brightened helpfully. "What about cereal and vitamins?"

Ten minutes later, they had yet to make much progress. The boys were still missing, and while the girls had seized upon the idea of making stew they had very little idea as to how to go about accomplishing such a feat.

What was worse, their antics hadn't gone unnoticed. They were attracting a bit of a crowd.

"There goes another one!" Molly hissed, pulling up her collar as she hurried the cart down the next aisle and out of sight. "I swear, this is not in my head. *Everyone* is staring."

"People always stare," Angel replied, flipping back her hair with a shrug. "They're like lemmings. It's just what they do."

Rae rolled her eyes, but she couldn't help but think that Molly had a point. It was like they couldn't go more than five steps without looking up to see someone else watching them from around the corner. From behind boxes. From the far end of the store.

It was getting kind of creepy.

"Oh, excuse me!" Molly apologized quickly, gazing up at a tall man she'd accidently backed into while trying to navigate the cart. "I didn't see you there!"

It was like running into a statue.

The guy said nothing. Not a single word. He just stood there, staring down at her, until she and the rest of the girls hurried on their way. His eyes followed their every move.

Yeah, definitely creepy.

"Hey, there you are." Devon rounded the corner suddenly, followed closely by Julian. "Are you guys about finished? We should probably start heading back."

It was said casually enough, but the way he kept glancing over his shoulder made the hairs on the back of Rae's neck stand on end. She abandoned the cart, and came to stand beside him.

"Are you starting to get the feeling that—"

"*Hey!*"

The four of them whirled around to see Julian staring in astonishment at a middle-aged woman who'd just grabbed his arm. She was one of those upper-class, velvet track suit women. The kind who usually didn't do her own shopping. The lipstick was perfect, every hair was sprayed into place, and her manicured fingers were closed in a taloned fist over Julian's jacket.

"Can I...can I help you?" Nothing happened. She didn't even blink. Casting a nervous glance over his shoulder, Julian gave his arm a tentative tug. Then another. Then he began to quietly panic. "Let go of me."

She didn't move an inch. She hardly even registered that he'd spoken.

"What the hell are you—"

"Let him go," Devon commanded, swooping in between them. "Seriously, lady, it's not funny anymore. Back off."

There was a soft rustling behind them, and Rae cast a secret glance over her shoulder to see that at least five other people had gathered to watch. They were all staring with that same blank, hungry expression. An expression that twisted her stomach with each passing second.

"Devon?" she whispered.

He cast a quick glance behind him before turning back to the woman. It was clear she wasn't moving. If anything, she seemed to be waiting for something. Just like the rest of them.

Instead of pushing her away he grabbed his friend, pulling Julian back with a burst of supernatural strength. What followed was the sound of ripping leather, followed by a sharp cry.

"What the hell?!" Julian gasped, staring down at his arm. The sleeve of his leather jacket hung in tattered shreds, ribboning to the floor, and a sudden rush of blood streamed down from the five large claw marks torn into his skin.

Rae and the others stared at it in shock. They lifted their eyes to where the woman was still standing exactly where they'd left her. Holding a piece of jacket in her hands. Her fingernails painted crimson with blood.

A single thought floated into her head, one that chilled her to the bone.

"When was the last time you heard Luke or Kraigan over the intercom?"

And just like that...the store of statues came to life.

Molly's head whipped around with a piercing cry as Angel flipped over the crowd and bolted off in the other direction, trying to find Gabriel.

"LUKE!" Molly screamed again. "LUKE!"

Devon pulled Julian back just as the woman lunged again. This time wielding a knife she'd snatched up from a cheese display. The blade sliced the air just an inch from where he'd been standing, and without another thought the four friends ran.

"What the freakin' A is going on?!" Rae shrieked as they ran, dodging shoppers left and right. A security guard with a night stick leapt out in front of her, and she knocked him to the ground before leaping over the body. "Devon, aren't these just—"

"People," he panted beside her, his eyes alight with panic, "these are just people."

On the far side of the store, the manager locked and bolted the door with an unnaturally solemn look on his face. The second he had, five or six other people started building a barricade of picnic tables and camping supplies.

"LUKE!" Molly couldn't stop screaming. No matter how fast she was running. No matter how many people were trying to get in her way. "LUKE! WHERE ARE YOU?!"

A burly man jumped right in her way but Devon punched him in the face and scooped her up in his arms, never breaking his stride. Her tiny arms wound around his neck as she stared in terror over his shoulder at the mob of people closing in.

It was endless!

One by one they came out of the aisles, took a second to get their bearings, then turned their heads and began shuffling forward. Moving in unnatural unison. Their blank faces and unblinking eyes unifying them like some sort of zombie horde.

Samantha.

Freakin' Samantha did this.

Even as she thought the name, Rae could have sworn a burst of wicked laughter echoed in her head. A high-pitched giggling that was gone before she could locate its source.

"Devon!" Julian shouted, pointing at a set of double doors. A grizzled-looking pharmacist caught him by the shoulder, but he yanked himself free. "The intercom should be in there, but I have to go back! I have to get Angel!"

Devon whipped around, almost doubling back himself. "Jules, no—"

But it was too late.

Julian dug in his feet and changed direction, sprinting straight back towards the ravenous crowd. The last thing Rae saw was his dark hair whipping behind him as he leapt a countertop and disappeared from view—vanishing without a sound in the center of the horde. "JULIAN!" she screamed.

It was like every one of her nightmares had come to life. Trapped in a building with no way out. Everyone she loved trapped inside with her, each of them in mortal peril.

Only this time there was an unexpected twist.

They couldn't fight back.

These people were inkless. Innocent. Local townsfolk of Kent. They had no idea that things like magical powers even existed in the world, let alone the fact that they were under a spell.

How could they raise a hand against people like that? How could they even defend themselves when every time they tried they were spilling innocent blood?

And as if that wasn't enough...what if the people were all programmed to remember?

Devon had remembered every single thing Samantha made him do over at Guilder. So did Luke. So did Angel. So did Keene.

Why would these people be any different?

No powers. No feats of strength or speed. No daring acrobatic escapes.

What did that leave them with?

"Devon," Rae gasped, taking great care to sprint at a human pace, "maybe we should—" She cut off suddenly as a man in a postal uniform stepped out from behind an arrangement of holiday cards, swinging a giant fist. With a startled cry she ducked beneath it, then pushed him with carefully measured strength back into the stationery.

A second later, he got right back up to his feet and started advancing again.

"Maybe we should call the police!"

"The police?" Devon panted, setting Molly down as he started working on the door. "You mean the common world police or the Council?"

"Either!" Rae looked in fright at the ever-approaching crowd. "Both!"

"I can't get this damn lock," Devon growled, battling impatiently against the door.

Molly whirled around, panicked beyond reason.

"Just kick it down!" she shrieked. "Luke's in there!"

Devon glanced warily at the mob before lowering his voice. "I shouldn't be able to—"

"DEVON!" A spray of erratic sparks shot out of her fingers as she banged her hand against the door. "I said LUKE's in there!"

The silent dilemma shadowed across his face for only a second before he nodded hastily and took a step back. A second later, the door fell away in shower of splintered planks. They barely had time to fall before Molly went clambering on through.

"Molls!" Rae cried, tearing after her. "Let me go in first, you're pregnant—"

A second later, a swinging baseball bat caught her right in the chest.

She flew backwards, tripping Devon behind her, gasping for breath as she collapsed to all fours on the cheap industrial carpet. She couldn't see Molly anymore. She was having trouble keeping track of anything going on around her. All she could make out was a quick rush of air as Devon leapt over her, followed by the sharp crack of his boots as he landed on the other side.

A second later, the bat was in *his* hand. The man who had swung it was out cold. And a granite countertop went flying over her head as he quickly barricaded the door.

"Are you okay?" he asked, helping her to her feet.

She tried to speak, but couldn't. It was hard enough to pull in a breath. "Molly," she choked. "We have to find—"

There was a crash in the other room, and the two of them took off running.

It was only then that Rae realized that it wasn't just her; Devon was having a hard time breathing as well. It wasn't something he seemed to notice, but there was a harsh, ragged edge to the way he was panting. This coming from a man who was never even out of breath.

Is the air thicker in here?! What the hell is going on?!

The second they rounded the last corner, they found the three missing members of their gang. And it was exactly as terrible as Rae could have possibly imagined.

Nightmare didn't even begin to cover it...

Chapter 16

Luke lay slumped unconscious over the table. Kraigan was bleeding from the head and tied to a chair. Molly was nowhere to be found. And the room?

The room was on fire.

"No! No, no, no!" Rae cried, leaping forward to drag her brother back as the roaring flames got closer and closer to his legs. The knots of rope binding him held firm, and after a minute of struggling she ended up dragging the entire chair. "Kraigan, you okay?! Wake up!"

On her other side, Devon was working on Luke.

"I don't know what's wrong with him." His voice shook with panic. "He's not bleeding, there are no visible wounds. I don't..." Then he spotted the empty syringe lying on the floor at the same time Rae saw it. He bent down and picked it up with a look of utter horror, turning it over with trembling hands. "...Rae."

She looked down at Kraigan long enough to make the connection, then at Luke. Sure enough, there was a tiny puncture in Luke's neck. An almost imperceptible cut around which a bruise was already forming. All the color drained from her face as she slowly got to her feet. "Does he have a pulse?"

Looking almost too afraid to check, Devon reached out two fingers and pressed them as gently as he could onto Luke's neck.

Rae's breath caught in her chest and she stood there, not moving, not breathing, as the rest of time seemed to stand still.

Then Devon gasped in relief and the world started up again. "It's faint," he breathed, "scary faint. But it's there."

Rae put her hands on her knees, taking deep, steadying breaths. "Thank freakin' goodness."

"Luke." Devon started shaking him gently, untying the knots that bound him with his other hand. "You've gotta wake up, man. We've gotta go."

Rae left him to it, and glanced around for something she could use to free Kraigan. It was only then that she heard the tiny sob from inside the closet. Quickly wheeling her brother away from the flames, she darted across the room and threw open the door. "Molly!" She sank to her knees at once, gathering up the sobbing girl in her arms. From the looks of things she was severely shaken, but unhurt. And by the angle at which she was slumped against the floor, there was a good chance she had taken one look at Luke, and fainted dead away.

"Is he...? Is he...?" Her blue eyes roved wildly over Rae's shoulder, seeing but not seeing all at the same time. "I couldn't even check. I couldn't—I couldn't breathe. I can't—"

"He's okay, I promise." Rae pushed the crimson hair out of her face, streaking the smudges of soot that clouded her friend's fair skin. "Devon's with him now. He's got a pulse."

To be honest, she was almost more worried about Molly at this point. Her eyes were dilated almost completely black, and there was a manic detachment to the way she was staring around. No matter how many times Rae tried to steady her waves of full-body trembles were chattering her teeth, and though she didn't seem to realize it herself one hand kept clutching at her stomach. "Molly..." She lowered her voice soothingly, trying to ignore the scorched beams that were crumbling in the breakroom beside them. "Luke is going to get up and leave now. Are you ready to come with him?"

Perhaps it was the odd phrasing that finally got Molly's attention. Her head jerked back to center as she focused on Rae for the first time. "Yeah...I'm ready to go."

"Good." Rae flashed her a quick smile and helped her to her feet. As she took a silent moment to steady herself, Rae glanced over her shoulder at Devon. "Please tell me you got him up."

"Working on it..." Devon was still kneeling on the floor, trying to tune out the flames as Luke's head stirred weakly against his chest. Every breath was labored, and every movement was painfully slow. "That's it, buddy. You got it. Open your eyes for me, okay?"

Luke was trying, but whatever drugs he'd been given were still fresh in his system. The room with the intercom was unfortunately right next door to the pharmacy, so there really was no limit as to what potential combination might be racing through his veins. "...Smoke," he mumbled, trying and failing to open his eyes. "I smell smoke."

Devon glanced around in a mild panic, trying not to let it seep into his voice. "Yeah, the room is kind of...the room is on fire. That's why we've got to get going, okay?"

If he were to simply pick Luke up and carry him out, they would be overtaken in seconds by the crowd. The guy had to come out of it on his own. And he had to come out of it fast.

For that matter, so did Kraigan.

Now that Molly was standing on her own, Rae turned her attention back to her brother. He was still passed out cold in the chair, but unlike Luke she didn't think he'd been given any drugs to make it happen. If the wide gash dripping blood down the side of this face was any indicator, it looked like he'd been hit with something instead. Judging by recent experience, Rae was going to guess it was a baseball bat. "Hey," she shook him roughly, kicking his shoes at the same time, "wake up! Come on, Kraigan! Wake up!"

Nothing happened. He didn't even stir.

In desperation, she ripped off a piece of her sweater and dipped it in the fire. The flames curled around the fabric before she stomped it out, holding the charred piece beneath his nose. "Come on, Kraigan! You can do this. I know you can."

The smell roused him and his body jerked awake. He smacked it away automatically before blinking around in a bit of a daze. Looking first at the fire. And then at his sister.

"What happened?" He tried to stand up, but he was still tied to the chair. "Is this...? How did...?" His eyes focused on her all at once. "Did you do this?!"

The moment of brother-sister bonding shattered in an instant.

"No! You ungrateful little bastard! *I* did not do this!" She pushed to her feet and started working again on the knots, muttering angrily under her breath. "Should've just left you here..."

A second later, the last of the rope fell free and he sprang from the chair. Eyes darting around. Ready for anything.

A few steps away, Devon was helping Luke get shakily to his feet. "That's it," he encouraged softly. "You've got it."

A wave of nausea swept through him, and Luke bowed his head painfully to his chest. "My dad...can you call my dad?" His voice shook with every word, and his legs seemed in no condition to support him. "Dev, they're just five minutes away."

A strange shadow flickered across Devon's face at the word 'dad' but he brushed it off quickly, throwing Luke's arm around his shoulder instead. "Everyone who walked into this store tonight is trying to kill us," he said quietly. "I don't know if we want to be inviting people with powers to walk inside, too." His glanced across the room and locked eyes with Rae. "The same thing goes for the police. The police carry guns."

He was right. There was nothing more to be said.

With a shaky nod, Rae put an arm around Molly and pulled her closer to the group. "So, what's the plan, then? Even if we can make it out the doors and to safety, we can't leave all these people inside—the entire place is coming down in the fire."

Molly left her side in a blur of crimson hair, throwing her arms around Luke. "I don't care," she muttered. "Let's just go."

Devon watched her for a second, then bowed his head sadly. "You will care. You'll wake up tomorrow morning and you'll care. We have to do something to get them out."

"Something like what?" Kraigan demanded. He seemed far less upset about the fact that they were being besieged by an angry mob than he was that someone in that mob had gotten the jump on him. "In case you've forgotten, they're all trying to kill us."

As if to echo his sentiments, there was a sudden pounding down the hall. The gang ventured to the doorway to see the granite table they'd used to barricade themselves crack up the middle as it was struck with a dozen angry fists. Another crack started up along the side. It was only a matter of time before the entire thing gave way.

Kraigan raised his eyebrows doubtfully, and Rae punched him in the arm.

"I don't care. We get them out," Devon said firmly. "And we go right now." His voice dropped an octave, twisting with fear. "Julian's out there..."

Without another word, the five of them headed for the door.

But they hadn't gone more than a few steps when there was a broken gasp as Luke's legs gave out beneath him. "I can't go with you..." he panted. "I'm just going to slow you down."

"Don't be ridiculous!" Rae exclaimed, rushing around to take his other arm. "Of course you're coming!"

He pulled away. "You're going to have to fight your way through each one of those people, knowing that they're trying to kill you but you can't hurt them. And on top of all that, the building's on fire."

There was a steely resolve in his voice that chilled Rae's blood. A grim hardness to the set of his face that made her want to run right back into the closet.

"Get Molly out. Keep her safe. Try to put back the door when you're done," he said to Devon, trying weakly to reclaim his supported arm. "With any luck, the fire department's already on their—"

"Are you kidding me?"

The room fell momentarily silent as Molly came to stand right in front of him. Her arms were folded in front of her chest, and she had apparently snapped all the way out of her shock-induced trance because Rae had never seen her so serious.

"Molly," Luke's entire body ached with the name, "there's no time, love. They all know that I'm right. You guys make a run for it, and I'll...I'll try to hold them off as long as I—"

"Luke Armistead Fodder. If you say even another word, I'm going to kill you myself." Her eyes flashed electric blue as she glared up at him, standing toe to toe. "You no longer have the option to try to sacrifice yourself. You gave up the right to be selfless when you told me you loved me. So I'm going to tell you what you're going to do."

She spoke in a tone Rae had never heard before. One that commanded the entire room.

"You are going to stay on your feet. You're going to leave this damn grocery store. You're going to be a father to this baby. And you are going to marry me."

A ringing silence followed the commands. One that grew louder with each passing second.

Then Luke took a wavering step forward. "Are you asking me to marry you?"

There was a beat.

"...*Now*?"

Molly blushed slightly, but held her ground. "It's more like I'm telling you."

Luke's mouth fell open and he blinked in shock, suddenly oblivious to the fact that the fiery room was coming down around them. There was a split second of silence then, despite the fact that they were all surely about to die, a little smile sparkled in his eyes.

It was a smile that Molly was quick to reciprocate. Smoke-smeared face and all. "Is that a yes?"

He grabbed her the next instant, scooping her up in the world's most perfect kiss. It went on for almost a minute, and by the time he set her down they were both out of breath. "That's a yes."

A tiny squeak of excitement burst from her lips, and without thinking her hands flew again to her stomach. But just as quickly she sobered back up, looking impossibly stern. "Well, you have to leave this room to do it."

That ended the discussion of whether Luke was going to stay. Looking like the deadly trip to the grocery store had somehow transformed into the greatest night of his life he threw his arm back around Devon's neck with a vengeance, bracing his feet against the ground. When they were both ready to go, Rae and Kraigan stepped out to take the front while Molly fell back to the rear.

"Remember, no powers," Devon said softly. "They don't know what they're doing, but they'll remember this all in the morning." His eyes flickered quickly between Luke and Molly before a little smile flashed across his face. "And congratulations, guys. When we get home, we'll celebrate. I've got a nice bottle of Scotch saved for a special occasion."

Rae flushed with a mix of absolute fear and utter joy, while Kraigan simply shook his head.

"You are the weirdest freakin' people I've ever met."

A second later they ripped down the door.

Chapter 17

It was complete and utter chaos inside the store.

The likes of which Rae had never seen.

She'd been in battles before. In her young life, she'd already seen more than her share. However, for whatever reason, those didn't really compare.

Probably because all those battles had had two sides. One fighting for good, and one fighting for evil. There was a clear winner and a clear loser. And when the dust settled, the battle was done.

But if there was one thing Rae knew for certain as that granite wall crashed down and the five of them launched themselves into the fray, it was that no one was going to leave this place a winner. And even after the dust settled, she was afraid the battle was just getting started.

"Rae—behind you!"

In the time they had taken to recover their missing friends, the people in the grocery store had had a chance to organize themselves. They were armed now—in a manner of speaking.

Armed with things like kitchen knives and gardening equipment. But it was armed nonetheless.

Rae threw up an arm to block the pair of pruning shears that swung her way. *"Freakin' A!"*

They caught her squarely in the arm, slicing deep into her skin. Under normal circumstances, they would never have touched her. She knew at least five different blocks that would have turned the blade right around on her opponent.

But all those blocks would have injured the elderly grandfather swinging those shears to quite a serious extent. And with Luke huddled protectively inside their circle, it wasn't like she could just dodge it by springing away.

"Are you okay?" Devon shouted over his shoulder, trying to combat a trio of cashiers who were stabbing at him with steak knives. "Rae, talk to me!"

Rae straightened painfully, bracing herself for the next round. But before the old man could wind up to swing again, Kraigan flew out of nowhere and knocked him off his feet.

Rae stifled a gasp as the old man landed on the floor with a little crunch, but even from where she stood it was easy to see that her brother had done no lasting damage. He'd simply knocked the man unconscious, then kicked him out of the way.

"Yeah," she gasped, lowering her hands in surprise, "I'm fine." The fighting continued, but between blows she cast a glance at her brother. "Thanks, Kraigan."

"No problem," he panted, ducking under a rolling pin. "What's family for?"

She kicked a hefty stockbroker right in the chest, and sent him flying back into a pyramid of canned soup. "Careful. You're starting to sound like dear ol' Dad."

A bark of laughter shot out of Kraigan's mouth, one cut only slightly short when that same woman with the rolling pin caught him right in the throat. "Hey! You were the one who wanted a more normal home life." He spat out a mouthful of blood, and used a can of minestrone to bash the woman over the head. "Now you've got one."

"Let's keep it moving, you guys!" Devon shouted. "The last time we saw the others, they were headed to the far side of the store!"

As a group they started moving as fast as they could across the tiles, slipping on food and spilled cartons of eggs and juice as they went. From a distance, it might have looked like the entire place had simple erupted into an especially violent food fight. Had it not been for all the smoke curling into the air.

...and the blood.

"That doesn't look good," Luke murmured, picking up the pace. Whether it was due to Molly's spontaneous proposal, or simply the fact that the drugs were starting to wear off, he was moving much faster now. By the time they got to the other side of the store, he was standing shakily on his own two feet. "This doesn't look good at all."

Molly spun around in a circle, scanning every which way she could. "Where the hell are they?" A wave of panic tightened her throat. "We didn't pass any more employee rooms along the way. There's nowhere else for them to go."

Devon's eyes flashed to the streaks of blood staining the white linoleum before he threw back his head with a deafening shout.

"JULES!"

In unison, the others echoed his frantic cries.

"JULIAN!"

"GABRIEL!"

"ANGEL!"

The mob had almost caught up with them by now. If it weren't for the fact that they'd been running faster than was permitted, they'd be upon them already. As it stood, they only had a few seconds. After that there would be nowhere for *them* to go.

"JULIAN!" Devon yelled again, straining to see over the tops of the broken shelves and collapsed wine racks. "JULES!"

It was then that they heard it. The sound of distant shouting. The sound of frantic screams.

The gang took off the next second, sprinting as fast as they could without any thought as to powers or exposure. Devon, who had warned them of the repercussions, was leading the pack. Less than a minute later they got to the front of the store, only to stop dead in their tracks.

Julian, Angel, and Gabriel were all alive. That much was clear.

...but that was about the only good thing you could say about their present situation.

To start, all the blood on the floor clearly belonged to them. There was hardly an inch of skin that wasn't torn open or abused in some way. From light bruises and tears, to full-out breaks and lacerations. From the way Angel was cradling her left arm, it was surely broken. Julian had what looked like three shards of glass sticking out of his ribs. And the entire left side of Gabriel's body was covered in a massive burn.

They had clearly tried to run for the front door when things started looking dire, but were slowed down by the massive barricade. Then came the fire. Then came the rest of the mob.

As it stood, they were standing on their last legs. Their movements had become instinctual, imprecise. Lashing out with rash strikes that spoke to blood loss, not training. They were back to back, protecting each other as much as they could. But they were trying simply to defend, and everyone around them was playing for keeps.

Every time they'd stop one attack, two more would spring up in its place. And every time they knocked someone down, they would get right back up on their feet and come back for more.

They hadn't yet noticed their friends, standing half-hidden by the shelves. But judging by the looks of things it was only a matter of time before they'd be overwhelmed completely, and lost.

Devon took one look at them and then, like a seasoned general, he started giving out orders.

"Molly, Luke, Kraigan, you guys try to tear down that wall in front of the door. We're going to need to get people out of here before the fire catches up." They nodded and took off running while he held out a hand to Rae. "You got another fight left in you?"

Her fingers closed around his as a look of bloody determination flashed through her eyes. "I thought you'd never ask."

With a mighty cry they launched themselves straight into the middle of the fray, taking the mob by storm as they started forcibly removing people one by one. Julian looked up in surprise, while Angel collapsed back against the barricade in utter exhaustion.

For his part, Gabriel took down three people at once with a dented hairdryer before flashing Rae a quick wink. "About time you got here. Thought I was going to have to do it all by myself."

Rae let out a breathless gasp of laughter as she and Devon fought their way through the mob to join them. Leaving a trail of unconscious bodies in their wake.

"Hey, man," Devon looked Julian up and down, simultaneously throwing a man trying to jump him into a row of potted plants, "I say this as a friend...you look like shit."

Julian laughed painfully, using one man's body to topple another. "Yeah, well, while you guys were off shopping for risotto some of us were here, fighting off Kent's very own zombie apocalypse."

Devon flashed him a quick grin. "You know there's, like, an entire window sticking out of your chest, right?"

Julian grimaced, glancing down at the pieces of glass. "Yeah, I've decided to leave it."

On their other side, Rae and Gabriel were making short work of the rest of the crowd. They might have been faltering before but the wave of reinforcements had revitalized them both, propelling them to new heights of determination as they knocked people out one by one.

"What about you, Kerrigan?" Gabriel panted, spinning around in a flying kick so fast it left Rae breathless. "You taking this opportunity to make any deep life revelations?"

A flying trowel spiraled towards her, and she caught it with one hand. "Yeah," she hurled it behind her at the windows, shattering the glass, "I've decided never to try to make dinner again."

He chuckled briefly, then they both lifted their heads to watch as the clouds of smoke that had been slowly enveloping them siphoned out into the cool night air. It was a good strategy, one that bought them all a little bit of time, but it wasn't going to last. The entire place was coming down in flames, and if they stood any chance of getting these people out they'd have to move. *Now.*

"How's it coming with that door?" Devon called over his shoulder.

Behind him, the others were almost through to the other side. Another minute or so, and they'd have created an opening.

"Sixty seconds," Molly shouted. "Then we're home free!"

Home free might be overstating it a little. What about the rest of the people?

It was as if she'd spoken out loud.

"Rae."

Julian called out softly, but she still heard him loud and clear. The two of them took a momentary step back as the others filled their spots.

"All these people..." His dark eyes swept over the scattered bodies, lying helpless and vulnerable in various states of sleep. "You don't want all that blood on your hands. Trust me."

Their eyes locked, and she understood.

With a firm nod she turned back to Devon, who was just taking down the last of the two civilians still moving. "Dev, we've got to get these people out."

His dark hair swung into his face as he dodged a frying pan, but one strategic kick later he straightened back up as the coast was finally clear. "Yeah, babe, I was planning on it."

"No..." she put a hand on his arm, "we need to get *all* these people out."

He stared at her for a moment before turning to gaze around the rest of the store. At this point, there were over a hundred bodies scattered all over the entire premises. Not to mention the man they'd left unconscious outside the breakroom door.

Getting them all out to safety might mean losing some people of their own.

"We have to," Rae whispered, squeezing his wrist as her eyes teared up with smoke. "It's our responsibility. It's the right thing to do."

"It's also probably suicide," Gabriel interjected quietly.

Devon pulled in a quick breath, gazing up at the quivering beams holding up the roof, before his shoulders fell with a silent sigh. "Yeah, but that doesn't mean we're not going to try."

As if on cue, there was a sudden cheer from behind them. The last of the barricade fell away, and a gust of freezing air swept inside as Molly and Kraigan kicked down the doors.

Julian turned to Rae and raised his eyebrows. "Well?"

She pulled in a deep breath. It was now or never.

"Alright guys!" she shouted, raising her voice above the roar of the fire. "We're going to get as many people out as we can! Start with whoever's closest and work your way back!" Her dark hair whipped around her as a strange buzz started vibrating her skin, like the flames of her own were just waiting to burst forth. "Fast as you can, guys! *Let's go!*"

There was something bizarrely counterintuitive about repeatedly running back into a burning building. Over the next twenty minutes, Rae did it so many times she lost track.

Again and again she made the treacherous journey, darting back into the scalding heat of the fire only to emerge a few minutes later with another person draped in her arms. She would lay them down in the parking lot, take a half-second to catch her breath, then run straight back inside.

But she wasn't the only one working. She had seven people working beside her. Seven people running into the fire by her side.

Never before had she been so exhausted. Never before had she been so proud. Never before had she been so flat-out terrified. All at the same time.

Every time the seven of them ran in, she was petrified that only six would come out. That while searching for bodies to rescue she would stumble across a familiar face instead. Twice she had almost seen it happen. Once when a broken beam fell upon Kraigan, and once when Molly got trapped behind a row of crumbling shelves.

But never once did they stop trying. Never once did they stop fighting the good fight. Again and again they ran inside until, finally, when there was not an ounce of strength left between them, the last of the people was dragged out into the lot.

The eight friends darted off quickly into the darkness, then collapsed in heap on the grass just as the fire trucks came screaming into sight.

"Perfect timing," Luke said dryly, his voice cracked with smoke.

"Seriously." Angel wiped a drip of blood from her ear as she nestled her head into Julian's shoulder, prepared right then and there to sleep. "Someone should give those guys a medal."

Julian laughed quietly, until that laughter turned into painful coughing.

At that point, Devon pulled himself back to a sitting position and angled towards his friend. "You still want to keep that glass. because I think it might be killing you."

The smile faded slowly from Julian's face, but by the time he realized what Devon was about to do it was already too late.

There was a blur of speed, followed by the loudest profanity that Rae had ever heard. A second later, the broken shards were lying on the grass.

"For the last time," Julian gasped, "you're *not* a doctor! I don't care how many classes you audited. Leave me the hell alone!"

Devon patted him on the back with an affectionate grin. "You're welcome."

The others chuckled softly then lapsed into silence, staring thoughtfully at the distant glow of the flames. One by one, they let the nightmare wash over them. One by one, they tried to emerge on the other side.

"I wonder why she did it," Molly finally said. Her hand was clutched tightly in Luke's, but her eyes were locked on the flames. "There are easier ways to kill us."

"Ways that don't involve so many innocent people," Devon added.

Rae bit her lip with a frown. The same thought had been looping through her mind since they dragged out the last person and made their escape. Instead she said, "How'd she know we'd decide to make dinner?"

But her thoughts trailed back to the questions her friends had asked. Samantha wasn't the type to delight in massive loss of life. Her designs were all based in revenge, and that revenge was very specific. This kind of move wasn't like her. She had to have something else up her sleeve.

"Maybe she did it to punish," Gabriel said quietly. "She didn't just start the fight, she started the fire. She couldn't have been counting on us to get all of the people out of there alive. She had to assume that there would be some collateral damage. That we'd have to live with it."

"Who the hell cares why she did it," Kraigan interrupted. "The girl's a psychopath. The things she does don't have to make sense. She does them because she's crazy."

Rae nudged him with a little grin. "You know, people have said the same thing about you."

"Like me," Molly piped up loudly. "I've said it."

"And me," Julian seconded.

Devon grinned. "And me."

Kraigan flashed each one of them a scowl before turning back to the fire. "The point is, I don't care about her motivation. She might have been trying to punish us. She might have just been messing with our minds—"

"—or she might have been trying to figure you all out."

An icy chill swept down Rae's spine. She knew that voice. She'd know it anywhere.

This time, the gang didn't even try to get up. Didn't try to fight the numbing influence that settled over their limbs as Samantha hiked up the hill and into sight. There were soot stains on her face as well, and judging by the red rims around her eyes she'd been watching for quite some time.

But something else was different about her as well, something that Rae was having a hard time putting her finger on. She looked...pleased.

"Maybe," she continued, "maybe she wanted to find out the truth about you. See if your moral compass really pointed north. Maybe she wanted to give you a little test. See if your allegiance to Simon Kerrigan was just a terrible fluke. See if you're good people deep down after all."

Rae's blood was boiling over in her veins. A hundred people were still lying in the freezing parking lot, and this deranged girl was speech-making about what it meant to be a good person?

No. I don't think so.

This night had been a nightmare come to life, and she'd had enough.

"You know, I really want to know, Samantha," she swiveled around as much as she could, glaring through the darkness with all her might, "what makes you so different?"

Samantha hesitated, and Rae viciously pressed forward.

"I'm serious. You're talking about a moral compass? Finding out if, deep down, we're all good people? The kind of heroes you always wanted? What the hell gives *you* any right to judge?" Her eyes narrowed with the deepest hate. She was the President of the Privy Council for a reason. She was Beth Kerrigan's daughter for a reason. These friends of hers risked their lives for a reason. Anger boiled inside of her. Samantha was just another Cromfield. "There were more than a hundred people down there. More than a *hundred* people could have died, all because you needed to prove a point." She shook her head, turning back to gaze down at the fire as the remnant of smoke stung her eyes. "You may think I'm a monster for not killing my father, you may think I'm the worst person on the planet, but let me tell you—I would never have done what you did tonight. Not in a million years." She gestured down to the parking lot. Even from up on the little hill, they could still hear the distant conversations. Still hear the painful groans.

"This is on you, Samantha. Not me, not them—*you*."

There was a long pause, then a little voice echoed out of the dark. "You're right."

The gang stiffened and turned as one to stare at Samantha.

She was gazing thoughtfully down at all of them, haloed by a ring of moonlight in the dark. "You're right. This is my doing, not anyone else's. And you were right about something else, Rae. Something you said back in your living room. Something I came tonight to see for myself." Her eyes flickered around the rest of the group, lingering for a moment on each one before softening almost imperceptibly. "They are...good people. Running in there again, and again, and again." She shook her head, a bit overwhelmed with the force of it. "They're not to blame for anything that's happened. I should have left them out of it. You were right when you said that. Because the problem isn't them. It's you." She turned away from the firelight and looked Rae right in the eye. "Which is why I'm going to take you away from them."

Before Rae could wonder what that meant, before she could even pull in a full breath, a wave of sleep came over her so strong it was impossible to fight it. Her eyes slipped shut in spite of herself as the impossible weight of the day crashed down upon her head.

Chapter 18

When Rae finally woke, hours later, the sky was just beginning to tinge with pink. The rest of them were still fast asleep around her, but as she pushed shakily to her feet they began to wake.

"What...the heck was that?" Molly asked, rubbing the back of her neck. "What happened?"

Luke stood up beside her, dusting off his pants. "I don't know. One minute, we were all just talking. The next, I was asleep."

"Devon," Julian gazed down the hill with a little frown, "isn't that your car?"

Devon pushed to his feet, shielding his eyes from the coming sunrise as he followed his friend's gaze. "Yeah. The one I got from Prince Phillip. What's it doing here?"

Rae stepped back in alarm, staring between them.

"What do you mean, what's it doing here?" she asked incredulously. "We drove it here last night. It was one of the three cars we took to go to the store."

Devon whipped around in surprise as those who hadn't been standing already leapt to their feet. They moved with such shock and urgency that Rae whipped around as well scanning the grass around her to see what had them so spooked.

"What is it?" she gasped. "Is Samantha still here? Did you see someone coming?"

There was a swish of air, then Devon was standing right behind her. "What are you talking about?"

She gazed up at him in shock. Had she miscalculated last night? Were they all more shaken up than she'd given them credit for? Maybe that beam really had fallen on his head. "*Samantha*," she said again, emphasizing it as much as she could.

"The girl who put us all to sleep after she lit the damn grocery store on fire. Devon, who did you think I was talking about?"

Devon's face lightened in surprise, and he took a sudden step back. "How do you know my name?"

Rae flashed him a grin, but it was a grin that was quick to fade. The rest of them were coming up behind him, standing in a defensive line as they surveyed the new threat.

A threat that Rae was just starting to realize might be her. "Come on," she said in a bit of a panic, glancing from person to person. "This isn't funny, guys. Samantha? The store? Last night?"

Devon shared a quick glance with Julian, who frowned and shook his head. When he looked back down, it was like he had never seen her before in his life. "I'll ask you again, how do you know my name?"

Her heart froze in her chest as she stared up into his sparkling eyes. "Devon, of course I know your name. It's me. Rae." She reached for his hand, but he pulled it away.

"I'm sorry...who?"

THE END
Glitch in Time
Coming – March 15

The highly anticipated Sequel to the Chronicles of Kerrigan series, by international bestselling author, W.J. May.

How do you fight for your world, when you're no longer a part of it?

As Samantha plays her deadliest card yet, Rae finds herself suddenly on the outside, looking in. Her friends don't know her. Her family doesn't recognize her. As far as the rest of the world is concerned, Rae Kerrigan doesn't exist.

Can she find a way back inside? How can she break through Samantha's spell? And more importantly....

Will she find a way to do it before her time runs out??

C.o.K Prequel Series

A Sub-Series of the Chronicles of Kerrigan.
A prequel on how Simon Kerrigan met Beth!!
Download for FREE:

PREQUEL –
- Christmas Before the Magic
- Question the Darkness
- Into the Darkness
- Fight the Darkness
- Alone the Darkness
- Lost the Darkness

The Chronicles of Kerrigan

Book I - *Rae of Hope* is FREE!
  Book Trailer:
  http://www.youtube.com/watch?v=gILAwXxx8MU
  Book II - *Dark Nebula*
  Book Trailer:
  http://www.youtube.com/watch?v=Ca24STi_bFM
  Book III - *House of Cards*
  Book IV - *Royal Tea*
  Book V - *Under Fire*
  Book VI - *End in Sight*
  Book VII – *Hidden Darkness*
  Book VIII – *Twisted Together*
  Book IX – *Mark of Fate*
  Book X – *Strength & Power*
  Book XI – *Last One Standing*
  Book XII – *Rae of Light*

The Chronicles of Kerrigan SEQUEL

Matter of Time
    Time Piece
    Second Chance
    Glitch in Time
    Our Time
    Precious Time

More books by W.J. May

Hidden Secrets Saga:
Download Seventh Mark part 1 For FREE
Book Trailer:
http://www.youtube.com/watch?v=Y-_vVYC1gvo

Like most teenagers, Rouge is trying to figure out who she is and what she wants to be. With little knowledge about her past, she has questions but has never tried to find the answers. Everything changes when she befriends a strangely intoxicating family. Siblings Grace and Michael, appear to have secrets which seem connected to Rouge. Her hunch is confirmed when a horrible incident occurs at an outdoor party. Rouge may be the only one who can find the answer.

An ancient journal, a Sioghra necklace and a special mark force life-altering decisions for a girl who grew up unprepared to fight for her life or others.

All secrets have a cost and Rouge's determination to find the truth can only lead to trouble...or something even more sinister.

RADIUM HALOS - THE SENSELESS SERIES
Book 1 is FREE:

Everyone needs to be a hero at one point in their life.

The small town of Elliot Lake will never be the same again.

Caught in a sudden thunderstorm, Zoe, a high school senior from Elliot Lake, and five of her friends take shelter in an abandoned uranium mine. Over the next few days, Zoe's hearing sharpens drastically, beyond what any normal human being can detect. She tells her friends, only to learn that four others have an increased sense as well. Only Kieran, the new boy from Scotland, isn't affected.

Fashioning themselves into superheroes, the group tries to stop the strange occurrences happening in their little town. Muggings, break-ins, disappearances, and murder begin to hit too close to home. It leads the team to think someone knows about their secret - someone who wants them all dead.

An incredulous group of heroes. A traitor in the midst. Some dreams are written in blood.

Courage Runs Red
The Blood Red Series
Book 1 is FREE

What if courage was your only option?

When Kallie lands a college interview with the city's new hot-shot police officer, she has no idea everything in her life is about to change. The detective is young, handsome and seems to have an unnatural ability to stop the increasing local crime rate. Detective Liam's particular interest in Kallie sends her heart and head stumbling over each other.

When a raging blood feud between vampires spills into her home, Kallie gets caught in the middle. Torn between love and family loyalty she must find the courage to fight what she fears the most and possibly risk everything, even if it means dying for those she loves.

Daughter of Darkness
Victoria
Only Death Could Stop Her Now
The Daughters of Darkness is a series of female heroines who may or may not know each other, but all have the same father, Vlad Montour.
Victoria is a Hunter Vampire

TUDOR COMPARISON:

Aumbry House—A recess to hold sacred vessels, often found in castle chapels.

Aumbry House was considered very special to hold the female students - their sacred vessels (especially Rae Kerrigan).

Joist House—A timber stretched from wall-to-wall to support floorboards.

Joist House was considered a building of support where the male students could support and help each other.

Oratory—A private chapel in a house.

Private education room in the school where the students were able to practice their gifting and improve their skills. Also used as a banquet - dance hall when needed.

Oriel—A projecting window in a wall; originally a form of porch, often of wood. The original bay windows of the Tudor period. Guilder College majority of windows were oriel.

Rae often felt her life was being watching through one of these windows. Hence the constant reference to them.

Refectory—A communal dining hall. Same termed used in Tudor times.

Scriptorium—A Medieval writing room in which scrolls were also housed.

Used for English classes and still store some of the older books from the Tudor reign (regarding tatùs).

Privy Council—Secret council and "arm of the government" similar to the CIA, etc... In Tudor times, the Privy Council was King Henry's board of advisors and helped run the country.

Made in the USA
Lexington, KY
06 April 2018